Rebels in the Shadows

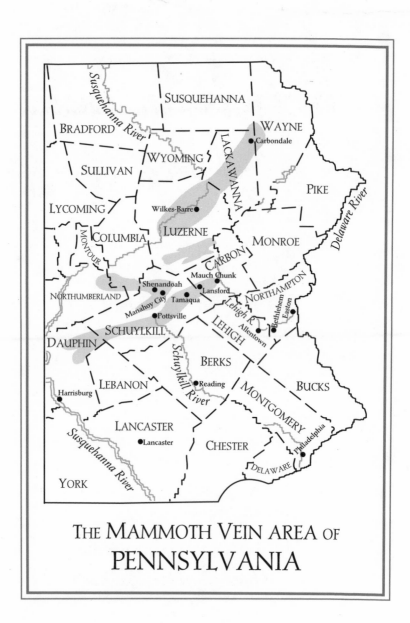

THE MAMMOTH VEIN AREA OF
PENNSYLVANIA

Rebels in the Shadows

ROBERT T. REILLY

Foreword and Afterword by
Margaret Mary Kimmel

Golden Triangle Books
University of Pittsburgh Press

A John D. S. and Aida C. Truxall Book

Published by the University of Pittsburgh Press, Pittsburgh, Pa. 15261
Copyright © 1962 by Robert T. Reilly
Foreword and afterword copyright © 2000 by the University of Pittsburgh Press
All rights reserved
Manufactured in the United States of America
Printed on acid-free paper
10 9 8 7 6 5 4 3 2 1

Library of Congress Cataloging-in-Publication Data

Reilly, Robert T.
    Rebels in the shadows.
    Reprint of the 1962 ed. published by Bruce Pub. Co.,
Milwaukee.
    SUMMARY: The violent activities of the Molly Maguires in the Pennsylvania coal
fields during the 1870's leave their mark on a family of Irish immigrants.
    [1. Coal mines and mining—Fiction. 2. Molly
Maguires—Fiction. 3. Pennsylvania—History—1865—
Fiction] I. Title.
[PZ7.R2746Rc 1979]   [Fic]   78-66069
ISBN 0-8229-5304-5

Contents

Foreword

The family of Mike Flannery lived and worked the coal mines near Pottsville, the center of the hard-coal fields of Pennsylvania in the turbulent era of the 1870s. Both Niall and Sean worked with their father–Sean as one of the "breaker boys," separating coal from slate, Niall deep in the mines, loosening the coal from the face of the mine wall with his pick. The work was dirty, backbreaking, and poorly paid; it was also very dangerous. If the mine didn't cave in, if there wasn't a fire out of control, the workers were still at the mercy of disease caused by the coal dust, poor diet, and marginal living conditions. Owners kept a fierce hold on the lives of their workers; the shacks they lived in and the stores they bought from were all under company control.

It is not surprising that these conditions gave rise to a group of militant workers, who called themselves the Molly Maguires. They were a secret society with passwords and codes of honor, seeking to right some of the terrible conditions of the miners. Theirs was a bitter fight, burning bridges and homes, beating the foremen and owners, even killing. The Coal and Iron police retaliated; injustice occurred on both sides.

The story of the Irish miners in the hard-coal region of

Pennsylvania is shared by many immigrant groups who were forbidden to unite in their demand for better working conditions.

Author Robert Reilly has long held an interest in Irish history and literature. He was born in Lowell, Massachusetts, on July 21, 1922, and has a graduate degree in English from Boston University. He was a lieutenant in the infantry during World War II, spending six months as a prisoner of war in Germany and earning many citations. After a successful career in business, Reilly held the Kayser Chair at the University of Nebraska, Omaha, where he taught courses in advanced writing, public relations, and Irish literature. His writing includes many articles and short stories and several books for young people, including *Red Hugh, Prince of Donegal,* which was the basis of the 1966 Disney movie *The Fighting Prince of Donegal.* The story he tells here of the Flannery family, Mike and Bridget, their children Kitty, Niall, and Sean, has been echoed in many different lives, but Reilly brings us a strong, vivid portrayal of a family living through perilous times.

Margaret Mary Kimmel

Preface

In the first years of the nineteenth century, anthracite, or hard coal, was discovered in eastern Pennsylvania, touching off a wave of immigration that rivaled the fabled gold rushes to the Rockies and the Yukon. Coal "patches," towns, and eventually cities emerged in the "Mammoth Vein" area of Schuylkill, Carbon, and Luzerne counties. It took a quarter of a century for anthracite to become popular but by 1830 it was fought over as a vast source of wealth and power.

For the poor people who streamed to the Pennsylvania hills the years brought disappointment. Unlike gold, coal could not be mined by the individual. It took money to get this mineral out of the ground and the poor man was there because he lacked money. Most of them stayed on and two distinct classes were formed—the mine owner and the miner himself.

England, Scotland, and Wales furnished most of the experienced men and to these men fell the highest positions. Hard labor was the lot of the Irishman and the German and the Slavic races that followed them. Working conditions were wretched. Hours were long and safety virtually ignored. The pay was extremely low and varied with the fluctuating demand. After paying his debts at the company store, the average miner found there was little of his monthly check left. He was in a state of constant impoverishment and only one level above slavery. The setting was ripe for revolt.

In the 1870's there were signs of revolution everywhere. The world was in turmoil with war, civil strife, the rise of Communism, the struggles of labor. Eastern Pennsylvania embodied these conflicts in miniature. Immigrant opposed native American; Protestant opposed Catholic; Irishman opposed Englishman; and Labor opposed Capital.

To combat the deplorable conditions, the miners began to organize into unions just after the American Civil War. For a time they made a show of strength but crumbled under the bitter opposition of the owners and their own lack of funds and leadership. The various nationalities were difficult to unite and a great many miners would not take the trouble to better their lot. Besides these difficulties, there was the overpowering presence of fear. Membership in a union could bring about unemployment, starvation, blacklisting in any mine in the country and, in many cases, long imprisonment.

Despite the demand for coal by the burgeoning new industries, the pattern altered very little. As wages dipped and more Irish labor flooded the area, the miner's life became more dismal than ever. Many of the smaller mines had been incorporated into single large companies owned by individual businessmen, by the railroads (which profited from the vein to the fireplace), or by large firms located at a great distance from the fields. The Civil War hastened the domination of these corporations. Since mining was a risky venture, these owners squeezed all they could out of the operation in the shortest possible time. And they kept their eyes peeled for "troublemakers."

In the face of this, the Irishmen turned to the device they had used for centuries—the secret society. Underground organizations sprang up under the banner of the "Buckshots," "Sleepers," or "Ribbonmen." The most infamous of these groups was the "Molly Maguires," named after an eighteenth-century band of native Irish rebels who terrorized landlords while disguised as women. Some authorities insist that no such group ever existed but that the name was invented by the mine owners to throw suspicion upon the whole body of labor. Later, the term was applied to strikers in New Jersey and to colliers in Ohio. It must be admitted that the evidence is clouded and much of the truth depends upon the credence which is given to personal and prejudiced testimony. But whether there was such a formal organization or not, the decade of the seventies was one of terror and violence with death being visited upon partisans of both sides.

Sometimes masked or acting under the cloak of darkness, these desperate miners would derail trains, burn collieries, threaten fellow workers, assault supervisors. Or they would lie in wait for a victim and dispatch him with a pistol shot. Cruelty provoked this cruelty and more cruelty answered it. Coal and Iron Police fired into mobs, burned dwellings, beat and imprisoned miners. Innocent men in both camps suffered.

How much of this can be blamed on the Molly Maguires? No one will ever know. But it is certain that many of the outrages for which they were accused were not the result of any formal crime syndicate but merely the natural consequence of savage living and working conditions.

A contemporary newspaper—one of the few which had any kind words for the miners—summed up the situation thus:

> It should be remembered, too, that the Molly Maguires were originally a band of decent men leagued together partly for political, partly for beneficiary motives, certainly not for robbery and murder. They belong to a people quick-witted, affectionate, devout. Yet they have sunk into brutes, because no adequate effort was made to keep them human. Nobody who has seen the coal miner close at hand can wonder that the utter stagnation and misery of his life makes whiskey or crime a relief to it. He lives and breathes in the coal, eats his salt pork, sleeps like the pigs, goes to work in the coal again. A few hardened ruffians thrown out of employment since the war closed found here good material to manipulate. Hence the Mollies and their murders. It is time they were manipulated differently.

By 1880 the era was closed. A score of men had been executed—some of them martyrs, no doubt. But the legacy of death and destruction was a long time in subsiding.

This is the story of those fiery years. This is the story of those dark days that spawned evil and hatred—and heroism. This is the story of the Molly Maguires.

Rebels in the Shadows

ONE

Fire and Death Below

*B*ridget Flannery shook the raindrops from her calico skirt and resolutely stepped into the muddy street. As she slogged along in her bare feet, a cloth sack hanging from her arm, she whistled between her teeth an Irish marching song. A stocky woman, with dark eyes and a tiny mouth, she combined a face full of youthful freckles with a mass of graying hair, tightly bound in a bun. The tune she whistled was grim and determined, like herself.

Overhead the clouds were dispersing, breaking into turbulent fragments and moving out of the mountains like an army in retreat. In the streets of Pottsville, lined with a monotonous row of red frame houses, the water ran black and sluggish. Down from a thousand gullies in the hills it rushed, past haphazard collections of drab miners' shacks which jutted from the slopes, past the neat brick homes of the owners, past the mounds of slate and into the ruts of the roads. Slowly the rain oozed into the mines, seeping through the wooden shoring, puddling the dark corridors. Grimy men cutting coal from the sides of the tunnels felt the cool drops and looked up, half grateful, half afraid. Then they continued their work mechanically, smashing picks and sledges into the black walls. Donkey carts rumbled by, hauling the coal to the surface. Up above, the water had diminished to a trickle and even this ended quietly in the swift moving Schuylkill River which bordered the town.

Mrs. Flannery mounted the porch of the company store and strode inside, not bothering to wipe her feet.

McDonald looked up from his ledger and frowned. Sarcastically, he greeted her. "Like the bogs of Ireland where you were weaned, isn't it, Mrs. Flannery?"

"And as black as the soul of a storekeeper," she countered, then turned her back on him to study the merchandise.

Momentarily checked, McDonald plunged back into his bookkeeping. A little soft fat man from Glascow, with square glasses surmounting a bulbous nose and ruddy face, he had managed the company store for twelve years. His hours were long, his tasks menial, and he had few friends. His store sold everything to the miner from gunpowder and pick handles to soap and clothing. Many mines made trade with the company store mandatory. All of them slyly suggested it as a good practice. Few regulations were more bitterly resented by the miners who often found the prices higher than elsewhere and who saw the store as a constant source of debt. Town stores were twenty per cent lower but the workers knew that failure to trade at the company store would mean dismissal when work got slack. So they paid a premium for such items as blasting powder, and as mining became more difficult they needed more powder. The owners claimed they kept the price up to discourage waste and to regulate the type used. The real reason was profit. This was mean work but McDonald was honest, cold, and efficient.

After a few moments of charged silence, Mrs. Flannery dumped her purchases on the counter—a few loaves of black bread, some beans, canned corn and tomatoes, salt pork, and a small package of stew beef.

"That will be all then?" McDonald asked curtly.

"With ten dollars a week in wages and your prices, it's all I can afford. And, sure, I wish I'd bought less."

McDonald flushed and tapped the register. His encounters with Bridget's sharp tongue always left him chastened. Still he persisted.

"I was noting, Mrs. Flannery," he said in his Lowland burr, "that your purchases have fallen off. Taking your trade elsewhere, I expect?"

Bridget regarded him as she would an impudent child. "What's that to you, man? Could I buy all me goods elsewhere, I'd not be lookin' into a face as has starved thousands."

"You're the saucy one, Bridget Flannery. You can keep a civil tongue in my place, I'll thank ye."

"Don't think to frighten me, Mr. McDonald. I'll not scare like some others. You may have most of me bobtailed check by the end of the month but you don't own me soul or tongue, so be writin' me down and I'll be on me way."

"If it weren't for your husband . . ."

"You leave Captain Mike out of this."

"Well, the Captain does know the rules and keeps 'em. No call to be buckin' the company, Mrs. Flannery."

"Why, it's you should worry, not meself." Bridget was smiling archly. "For I do hear the Mollies have marked you for their very own. Wouldn't it be the shame and all these fine things up in smoke." She shook her head in mock sympathy.

McDonald paled, then sputtered. "That's nothing to jest about, Mrs. Flannery. I'm a poor man—a workingman, like your husband. I've dealt squarely with them."

"Then there's nothin' to worry you." Bridget was still smiling. "But hurry, now. I'm off to me boy in the breaker."

"Aye." McDonald answered absently, but he tied the bundle quickly and stared after Bridget as she padded out of the store. Then he swallowed hard, bit on the stub of his pencil, and made a shaky entry in his ledger. Bridget slammed the door behind her, making him jump with alarm. Chuckling, she descended again to the street.

Less than a hundred yards away was the New York and Schuylkill Coal Company, its spindly shaft rising above the cluster of dirty frame buildings. A railroad spur dead-ended here and, to the rear of the mine, a long wooden chute led to the coal barges on the Schuylkill. Although the real work occurred below ground, there was—on the surface—a discordant chorus of activity. The droning exhaust fan removed foul air from the mine. The pump, chugging continuously, emptied the stagnant water. Blending with these sounds were the rumble of falling coal, the clacking hooves of the mules and the squeak of their carts, and, far below, the echo of the picks.

Mrs. Flannery stopped before the big black shed known as the "breaker." Here, in a room not twenty feet square, a hundred boys and a few old men straddled makeshift benches and picked out pieces of slate from the stream of coal that tumbled past them. As the vari-sized lumps came from the pits, they were deposited into chutes and roared into this room. The floor slanted so that the coal had a natural entrance and exit. At the top of the chute were the inexperienced boys. Below them were the old men and veteran youngsters who made the final check. Seated on the rough boards and coated with black dust, the breaker boys bent over their work in silence, banging away with their tiny mallets, gathering little piles of slate by their sides. Conversation was virtually impossible, due to the noise and the steady pressure of work. Hundreds of boys on the different shifts sweltered here in the summer and, bundled in rags, chattered in the chill blast of winter. In this room, thousands of lives had been warped and stunted.

At fifteen, Sean Flannery was one of the oldest boys in the breaker. Tall and thin, with delicate features encased in soot, he had already taken on a bit of the stoop that characterized the tired old men. In another year he would go to the pits with his father, Captain Mike, and his brother, Niall. His light blue eyes would still be ringed with black but he would be earning a miner's wage. Now he labored from seven in the morning until it was too dark to see and received two dollars a week. If things were slow, he sat outside the breaker and waited and received no money at all. There were no games here, no books. All Sean had to know was the difference between slate and coal. After six years, he knew this lesson well.

Across from him sat Brendan of Ballycotton. No one knew the old man's real name for, long ago, he had adopted the title of St. Brendan the Navigator as a grim sort of joke. His last forty years—after leaving his fishing village in Ireland—had been spent in this one mine. Coal dust streaked his long white hair and settled in every wrinkle on his leathery face. His back was bowed; his fingers gnarled and misshapen. But he

5

retained his spirit. Now he winked at Sean and the boy smiled, finding courage in the gesture. Sometimes Brendan would croak out an old Irish tune with himself as the only audience. Or, amid the din of the chutes, he would take up a sad miner's lament and make it sound like a carefree melody.

I'm getting old and feeble and I can work no more;
I have laid the rusty mining tools away.
For forty years and over I have toiled above the mines,
But now I'm getting feeble, old and gray.

I started on the breaker and went back to it again,
But now my work is finished for all time;
The only place that's left me is the almshouse for a home,
That's where I'll lay this weary head of mine.

In this way Brendan of Ballycotton shouted back at fate, forgetting his bent spine, his dusty lungs, his lost hopes.

The wooden door of the breaker swung open, admitting Mrs. Flannery with her sack of goods. Ignoring the bearded supervisor who stood over the boys with a willow switch, she made her way to Sean. Brendan nodded to her.

"It's the fine, brave worker you are, Brendan," she shouted.

He waved his hand at her. "Sure, I was never good at breakin' stones. Talkin's me great gift."

Bridget laughed as she knelt beside her son. She shouted in his ear. "There's bread here for ye and sausage your sister Kitty sent along. Tonight a stew will be waitin' on ye, so mind ye, Sean, and hurry on home."

Sean glanced around, embarrassed before the other boys. But they continued on, heedless of the visitor. Sean thanked his mother and received an affectionate pat on the head. It was a hard life, she thought, and not like the good days in Ireland before the famine with her brothers living clean and sleeping clean and eating well.

"Come along now, Mrs. Flannery," the super warned her.

She wrinkled her nose at him in derision but arose all the same and started out. Just as she reached the door, a bell clanged furiously outside. They all recognized it as the warning signal which pealed only in times of emergency.

Bridget stopped and clapped a hand to her mouth. "There's trouble in the mine. I've had the feelin' all day." She raced out the door, leaving it ajar.

The coal hurtled on, down the chute and past the benches. But the breaker boys had ceased work. They were listening. Down below were their fathers, their brothers, their friends. Some of them rose, straining to hear.

"Sit down there," the supervisor ordered. "Back to your benches now." He brandished his switch over Brendan.

Sean leaped to his feet, bowling over the super, and sprinted for the door. The others were up with a shout and following him. There was trouble in the mine and they must see. Standing water, perhaps, escaping gas, or the collapse of decayed timber. It could be fire, or an explosion, or the suffocating fumes of the "black damp."

Across the muddy flats to the main shaft raced the unruly mob of boys. A crowd had gathered already—wives, mine officials, comrades of those below. Smoke was curling ominously from the opening.

"Fire, Ma?" Sean came up to his mother's side.

She nodded. "On the second level, they say."

"Niall and Pa still down there?"

"Down there somewheres." She blessed herself.

The circle of watchers grew as the frightened village emptied all its houses. Sean's sister, Kitty, ran up, her blue eyes wide in terror. She was short, like Bridget, and had the dark head of the Flannerys. Her features were tiny; her manner quiet. She asked no questions but merely joined the others, silent and fearfully expectant.

Then they saw the chains and pulleys move. The cage was coming up. Everyone craned forward, tense, hopeful. Some prayed aloud; others wept. A thin smoky haze settled on them, turning the sober throng into a grotesque tableau.

Brendan came along and slipped his aged arm around Bridget's shoulders. "Don't be frettin' so soon. Likely it's a small fire and all will be well." He spoke without conviction and drew no response. Like the others, then, he watched and waited.

The lift came to the surface, revealing several dozen smoke-blackened men, coughing and rubbing their eyes.

"The whole south end's afire," one man cried. "Gotta get those men out. There's a hundred of them down there."

Oliver Taggart, the burly mine boss, stepped to this man and clutched him roughly by the shoulders. "How'd it start?" he asked.

"God knows," the man replied wearily. "Kerosene from the caps, maybe. Them timbers is goin' like paper, Mr. Taggart. You better get them men out quick!"

"Hang it, man, what about the water? They've tubs of it below. What's the matter with the buckets? First sign of smoke you come barreling up like green field hands."

The miner sank to the ground, panting. "It won't do no good. Fire's got too big a start."

A hundred yards away the air shaft door slammed open and miners from the top vein issued out, frightened but orderly.

"Kill that fan!" they shouted. "It's whippin' the blaze somethin' fierce." The exhaust fan ground to a halt.

Taggart collared one of the newcomers. "What's going on down there? Can you tell anything?"

"Nothing on our level," replied a wizened old miner. "But them boys below are catchin' it sure. You can hear them yellin'. Must be awful. Fire's between them and the air shaft. Only escape is the cage and some of them'll never make it. They're off in the side galleries. Holin' up, maybe. They're cut off, poor devils." He whimpered as he wearily sagged to a sitting position.

The crowd started to chant. "Get the cage down!" They pressed forward, menacingly. Before them formed the Coal and Iron Police, clubs raised, black boots planted firmly in the mud.

Taggart pounded one hairy fist into the opposite palm. Then he gestured angrily. "Get 'em out!"

The cage dropped again, clanking, squeaking. Now the watchers could feel the heat and hear the flames crackling below. The voices of the trapped miners reached them bringing more gasps, more tears. Down, down dropped the cage.

Kitty fell to her knees in the mire and began a rosary. Others joined her, praying quietly and with great fervor. Sean prayed with them but remained on his feet, his ears straining for every sound.

Taggart paced up and down before the shaft, disdaining the prayers and thinking only of his responsibility—the Pottsville colliery. Tomorrow there would be questions and

Mr. Franklin B. Gowen, the owner, would want the right answers. Taggart was a bull of a man, broad through the shoulders and with a thick neck and powerful arms and hands. His face was beefy and scarred; his nose flattened. Beneath bushy brows, his eyes were cold and cruel. He had struggled through the mines as a laborer, a miner, as pit boss and weight checker. His wife died young and he was childless and alone. He fought to stay alive. Where many officials short-weighted, sold jobs, or accepted bribes, he remained honest. And now he was mine boss—tough, primitive, cunning.

The cage reappeared and another load of miners tumbled from the platform. Women raced toward them, laughing and sobbing. Some collapsed in disappointment. Then the cage descended again. Its wooden floor began to char and the metal was hot to the touch.

On the second level, Mike and Niall Flannery waited with the others. They had plunged through the initial wall of fire and emerged singed but unharmed. Now they lay on their stomachs, their shirts ripped and the cloth patches held over their faces. The heat was suffocating and made the skin pop. Behind them the fire gained slowly, eating up the timbers in its advance, launching spears of flame and showering the men with scorching sparks. They could hear the agonized screams of men trapped in the inferno, They could hear the mules running madly down the galleries and braying pitifully. They could smell the burning flesh. Most of all, they listened for the sound of the cage, their link with life.

An ember dropped on Captain Mike, searing him like a branding iron. Niall reached over and beat it out. Father and son looked at each other and nodded wordlessly, telling each other that rescue was near. All about them the men writhed, muttering curses or fitful prayers. The air was thinning out so that each man sucked laboriously for every breath. The fire edged closer.

"It's like hell down here," one shrilled.

"Get us out," another cried. "Get us out." He pounded his fist on the pit floor.

The cage hit their level again and the men dashed for it. A six by sixteen foot enclosure, it was built for a maximum of two dozen men. Fifty tried to climb aboard. Fights broke out and men were flung back into the searing passage. There were moans and sobs of despair. Niall managed a spot but Captain Mike hung back, allowing the others to get on. Seeing this, Niall leaped off as the lift rose and rejoined his father.

Again the cage reached the surface. By now tiny flames were licking at its floor and the chain hoist was blazing hot. The miners scrambled off and rushed to their families. Bridget scanned the group anxiously. She bit her knuckles until they bled but she could not see her men.

Taggart surveyed the hoist and made a decision. "She can't make another trip with those chains. Secure the cage and get some water on it."

The angry mob pressed against the police cordon, screaming abuse and threats.

"There's more than twenty men left down there in that one spot," snarled a rescued miner. "They're waitin' to come up. That cage goes down—or by all that's holy, you go into that pit yourself!"

There were shouts of approval and the circle tightened. Taggart wavered a moment and then chopped down with his hand to signal another descent. If the cage hit bottom, it would take thousands of dollars and many weeks to repair. Taggart spat in the mud and turned away from the shaft.

The watchers cheered and then lapsed again into stunned silence. All one could hear above the heavy breathing was the terrible shriek of those red-hot chains. Puffs of smoke and balls of flame shot out of the opening. The chains groaned on. Then they stopped and the watchers knew the second level had been reached. If they could hold now for the ascent.

Slowly the hoist assumed the extra weight and pulled for the surface. Now the chains were sawing into the cage roof, hissing and smoldering. The lift itself was afire as it creaked upward. The roof appeared, then the aching faces of the miners. When it halted, they climbed off, some walking, others crawling. Bridget, Sean, and Kitty rushed forward to support Mike and Niall and to drag them away from the terrible holocaust.

"There now," said Captain Mike, as Bridget clung tearfully to him. "It's all over and not a scratch on either of us."

"Thank God, thank God," was all Bridget could whisper.

"That's the last of the lot," Taggart shouted. "Tie her down there and get some buckets on that cage!"

Water was flung onto the platform where it boiled and steamed.

"Some sand and planks over here! Quick now!"

Niall spun away from his family and confronted Taggart. "What the devil are you doin' there?"

"Doing, boy? I'm sealing the shaft. Otherwise the whole mine'll catch fire and we'll never put it out. Not in a thousand years."

"You'll cut off the air!"

"That's the idea, boy. No oxygen, no fire. You got a better one?"

Niall clenched his fist. "There's men down there still. You're sentencing them to death."

Taggart stared at him impatiently. "Likely they're dead already. My job is to save the mine."

Niall was a head taller than Taggart, but thin, like Sean. His muscles tensed and he started a left hand at Taggart's chin. But Captain Mike had moved in behind him and wheeled him about.

Almost crazy with rage, Niall protested. "Pa, they'll roast those men alive!"

Captain Mike shook his shaggy head dejectedly. "Taggart's right. There's no hope for them. Better this way in the long run." There were tears in his gray eyes.

Niall stared at his father and his anger slowly subsided. Then he turned to face the fiery shaft and slowly bent his head. "Mother of God, have mercy on them."

The planks were slapped into place and the sand tossed upon them, like loose earth on a grave. In minutes the shaft was sealed. As the fire sputtered out below, forty lives disappeared with it.

Some of the women sat by the mine for long hours. It grew dark and hope ebbed. Still they sat, peering sadly into the blackness and wondering why they sat there. Then their friends came and led them back to their homes, now strangely quiet and empty.

There would be no wakes and no wreaths on the doors. Only the keen in the long night and then morning again in the mines.

TWO

The Mollies Pay a Visit

*F*or a week the people of Pottsville waited and then they brought out their dead. It was grim work removing the charred bodies from the pit—some in attitudes of prayer, some reaching toward the exits, some sitting patiently awaiting death. Grim work—but it had to be done. "Bury the dead," the Church says. And, on a gray morning in spring, Pottsville buried them. The New York and Schuylkill mine was closed, not solely out of reverence, but to repair the damaged cage. Over the mass grave, Father Daniel McDermott read the simple services.

The priest was a young man and slight compared with most of his congregation. Born of a fine family in New England, he looked upon his parish as a mission assignment. But he skillfully combined courage and prudence in a region where both virtues were necessities. He looked over his thick glasses at the assembled miners. There was violence in their hearts and he knew it. One wrong word might incite them, one unhappy choice of text. *His* people. He loved and pitied them. But he could not encourage hatred and he could not involve the Church.

"The Lord's ways are not our ways," he said, "and we must not question His will. The Lord gives and the Lord takes away and, with Job, we must bless His name. For the Bible tells us, 'Man is born unto trouble as the spark flies upward.' Try to see the blessing in this hour of grief. Try to see the hand of Providence. And, if there is a wrong to be righted, let it be done by this same hand. These men buried here now travel a road of peace. Let that be your path, too. Kneel, now, and let us pray for the repose of their souls."

They knelt and they prayed and some departed with understanding. Others carried away what they had brought to the service—a bitterness which would soon erupt into fury.

Among the last to leave were the Flannerys. Mike and Bridget led the group, glancing alternately at the threatening sky and at the little knots of people disappearing down the country lanes. Sean followed, keeping step with Niall. Bringing up the rear were Kitty and Jimmy Boyle, her sweetheart. It was a silent procession with each member coveting his own thoughts.

In Kitty, horror and fear were uppermost. She pictured herself sobbing among the widows. And wouldn't life with Jimmy Boyle come to this perhaps? At least it would prolong the sufferings she had never accepted. Instinctively, she revolted against the dim structure with the sagging floor and leaky roof which was her home. Even the furniture repulsed her—a rough table and some benches, crude bedsteads made of square timber by the colliery carpenter, the dirty coal grate, the rooms separated by sacking. And a dollar a week in ground rent for this shambles. It was not complaint exactly, but more a sickening reluctance to extend the generations of agony.

Jimmy Boyle knew this. Like Kitty, he was quiet and temperate. Although about her age, his snub nose and wide eyes would give him perpetual youth. His home and his work were in the Storm Hill mines, thirty miles up the valley, but he was a frequent visitor to the Flannery household and welcome there for his soft-spoken, gentlemanly qualities. A native American and an orphan, he had been courting Kitty for three years—since he was twenty. But their plans were indefinite. He had no words to frame a proposal to share his miserable life. Still, all of his dreams had not been consumed in the pit. Sometimes he thought of a factory job in the cities or of a life on the frontier, despite the current Indian scare. This new life might be offered to her. Now he was anchored to the mines by his own need. In a year or two, though, things might be different. He pressed Kitty's hand and she turned her face toward him, forcing a smile. This was all they had—a walk in the black streets and only an eye for the green hills and valleys beyond.

"Wasn't it awful, Jimmy? The poor women and children."

"Don't think about it. It's over for them at least—the dead ones."

"But not for the living." She stole a look at him as they walked on.

While Sean could sense the whirl of emotions surrounding him, he couldn't quite puzzle them out. So he thrust his hands in his pockets and trudged along, matching strides with Niall, and kicking at stray pieces of slate. He idolized Niall. His older brother was more than flesh and blood. He was Sean's figure of manhood and his complex of daydream heroes. Together they had spent most of the happy hours in an unhappy existence. On a rare free day they might tramp through the Pennsylvania hills and spy on the wild creatures who lived there. Or they would fish in the mountains using a crude willow rod and light twine. Sometimes they'd merely squat on a glacial boulder in the cool pine shade and talk, unmindful of the misery that always waited upon their return.

Now, however, Niall was uncommunicative. His mood was dark and sullen. For months he had smoldered inside, resenting all wrongs, hating the transgressors. Pent-up anger was driving him to some unknown decision. He craved expression for it. He wanted to strike back.

"Be cool tomorrow anyway." Bridget interrupted him, reaching back to touch his hand and cheer him. Niall forced a slight smile.

With the instincts of a mother, Bridget summarized all their thoughts. Their grief was her grief and their pain hers as well. She kept this hidden for she knew that hope rode on her shoulders. Only Captain Mike's thoughts were beyond her understanding.

Michael Flannery was powerfully built for a man in his forties. His face was strong, the features sculptured, the aspect commanding. Only his misty blue-gray eyes and dark lashes were feminine. Since coming to America in 1858, his hair had turned gray like that of an Old Testament patriarch. He had been a farmer in Kildare, then studied for the priesthood until his family's struggle in the famine called him home. Although he never discussed this lost vocation, its mark was still upon him. This was true not only in terms of learning (he was one of the few miners who read books) but also in his attitude toward suffering and his friendly reliance upon God. He married in Ireland and Niall and Kitty were born there. When both parents and farm were lost, he left for America, earning steerage passage for his family while laboring as a deckhand. In the United States, like so many Irish, he drifted to the mines for the promise of wealth. Inexperienced, he began in the lowest posts. He never complained, and when he fought, it was always in self-defense. He was never beaten. After the first few engagements of the Civil War, Mike joined up. His education and his daring under fire brought him a commission within months. Several bloody battles later, he returned to Pottsville, wounded, and with the rank of Captain. When he had recovered, he dropped into the mines again, forsaking the role of leadership and accepting the mantle of pain and anonymity. War had sickened him and had marked him like the seminary. Now he could see the signs of a new conflict and it distressed him. Secretly he had saved some money in the hope of some day leaving the Mammoth Vein country and returning to the land. This was his plot against poverty. He'd teach Niall to plant and harvest. Sean could tend the stock. Kitty would be married, certainly, and there'd be room for a willing hand like Jimmy Boyle. A perfect plan—and nothing was going to upset it. Not the hard days underground and not the hot blood in men's hearts.

When they reached the concentration of drab shacks, where their own home stood, a trifle larger than the rest and in better repair, it had started to drizzle. Two men were seated on their porch, waiting. Mike recognized them as Jake Roarity and "Powder Keg" Kerrigan. Both were miners from other parts of the valley and leaders in the Ancient Order of Hibernians, a militant society of Irishmen. Although Mike cared little for either man, he was naturally civil to everyone.

"Good evening, gentlemen," he greeted them. "You waiting for me?"

"If you have a moment, Captain Mike," said Kerrigan sweetly. A short man—barely five feet tall—Kerrigan was well proportioned and a dandy in dress. Abandoned by his father after his mother's death, he would later desert his own wife and children. He had an evil reputation for drinking and fighting. Like Mike, he was a veteran and possessed a fine war record. His nickname of Powder Keg, however, derived from a peacetime exploit. Denied a seat near an open fire on a wintry day, Kerrigan carried a powder keg to the center of the blaze and sat on it. When the other miners scattered, he withdrew the keg and sat down in comfort.

Roarity was an older man, gruff and illiterate, but with a natural grasp of relationships with other men. He was dedicated to a redress of the miners' wrongs and his forcefulness had placed him at the head of Coaldale's malcontents and spread his reputation down the valley.

"Would you care to come inside?" Mike asked them.

"Rather stay here, Mike, if it's the same to you," responded Roarity.

"Certainly." Mike waved the family inside, except for Niall who hung back. Mike did not exclude him. Father and son sat on the small porch, their backs against the wall, as Roarity addressed them. He was nervous in his anxiety to impart the right impression.

"Captain, I expect you're as sick as us over the death of them men in the mine," he began.

"Of course."

"We knowed you'd be," said Roarity, gaining confidence. "That's why we come thinkin' you'd join us. It's the truth we could use a man like yourself."

Mike frowned slightly. "Join you in what, Jake?"

"Come now, Mike, you know what we mean," said Kerrigan. "In the organization is what. There's still some men left in these hills—men who won't sit quiet any longer. We're askin' you to share in the fight that's shapin' up. You're a scrapper and you got the head for these things. You got the experience, too. What do you say?"

Captain Mike shook his head. "I'll have no part of the Molly Maguires."

Kerrigan feigned surprise. "Who used the word? Not me, Mike. A group of soldier fellows like yourself, I'm meaning, Mike. Men of character."

"Hah, soldiers, are they? Like as not they were dragged to the wars in chains or they hid in the hills when the call went out."

"You got it all wrong, Mike," Roarity protested.

"No, Jake. I don't believe in the killin's and the burnin's and the bloodshed. And I don't hold with secret societies and I want no part of the scheme."

"There's killin's on both sides, Captain," Kerrigan slyly interjected. "You know the blacklegs done their share of beatin'. And who burned out the Wiggan's patch and killed women and children but them blackleg police and the 'sheet iron' gangs sent by Gowen?"

"So you'll answer killin' with killin'? That's why Henry Dunne was shot, I suppose, and Morgan Powell? And that's the reason for the trains bein' blown off the tracks and the collieries fired? You've not sinned lightly in this yourselves."

Roarity interrupted. "Wait up, Captain. This ain't going to lead nowheres at all." He cleared his throat before continuing. "My feelin's simple. We works for near nothin' to begin with. Then the store gets most of that. We live like pigs, eat poorly, see our families sicken and die. Half a them graves in Coaldale and Mahanoy City and here in Pottsville, Mike, is kids' graves. You know that."

"I know it."

"We ain't been too successful in politics of late. The old man in Harrisburg ain't strong for us like it used to be. And now the war is over, wages is dropping again. Squeak about it and you're out of work, not only here but anywheres. Blacklisted in any mine. And you can't organize peaceable or the same thing happens. That's why the secrets, Mike. Protection."

"Years back, others found a way. And without bloodshed." Kerrigan sneered. "And where are they? What did they change? They died is what. Then unions died and things got worse. Now the big owners is in and they got us whipped. At least, some of us. Come on, Jake. Sure, we're wastin' our time on the likes of himself."

"Hold on, Powder Keg," Roarity ordered. "Mike, you have a family. So do I. So does Kerrigan here. You want them to live like we done—scared, stuck in these shacks, grubbin' for food, never havin' nothin' of their own?" He paused and concluded quietly. "It'll just be until we can make them owners see the sense in it. Then it'll be peaceable again and better for all of us."

"Jake, Jake," Mike said, shaking his head. "Blood never solved anything. You heard Father McDermott today. It's the path of peace we should be treading, not your route. Not the Mollies."

Kerrigan glared at Mike. "Next you'll be sayin' he was right about the will of the Lord and all. Him with his fancy upbringing' and quotin' the Bible."

"It *was* God's will. All deeds are in His keepin'."

Kerrigan lost control. "And I say it's not the Lord but Franklin B. Gowen. Maybe be *thinks* he's the Lord, but he ain't."

Captain Mike arose and cut him short. "I'll not have blasphemy here, not in my presence."

Roarity interrupted again. "Sure, Mike. Powder Keg don't mean no harm. He's only sayin' that if Gowen would've fixed them galleries with more exits and if he'd done somethin' about them fans, nothin' would've happened. They make them safety laws in Harrisburg but they don't mean nothin' in the coalfields. Gowen's boss here. You know that for a fact, Mike."

Kerrigan pressed on, angered and explosive. "He's out to do us all in, is your Franklin B. Gowen. A lot he cares, sittin' snug in his fancy home. All he knows is shortweightin' coal and workin' men to death. All he sees is coal. He don't mind no men nor care if they live or die. Taggart's like him. He does what Gowen says. They kilt them men last week sure as if they had guns."

Mike answered evenly, politely. "I'm no friend of Taggart but he has a difficult job. It takes a hard man to do it."

Kerrigan spit over the rail in disgust and turned to Roarity. "Let's go. There's no stomach for fightin' here."

"A minute. What about Niall here, Captain? He ain't spoke a word."

Mike shrugged. "Niall's of age. He's his own man. But I think he stands with his father."

Niall arose slowly, uncomfortably. "No, Pa, you're wrong. I'm for joining up with the others. The young fellers been talkin' about this for months."

Mike checked his disappointment. "This isn't the way, Niall. It will never be the way. Killin' and bloodshed. They'd make a murderer out of you."

"Pa, I've thought about it and my mind's made up. I'm tired of runnin' every time there's trouble. I'm a man and I want to act like one."

There were tears welling in Mike's eyes as he faced Niall. "And your father's no man, is that it, son? Niall, you know that I love you. You're the oldest, our firstborn. But if you follow these men you must do it all the way. There'll be no room for you here, no welcome. Not now or ever again."

For a moment their glances held, neither man yielding. Then Niall spoke. "I'm sorry, Pa. I'll be goin' then." He went into the house to gather his few belongings.

Mike stared after him briefly, then spun on the two miners. His voice was quiet but there was menace in his tone. "Get off my porch—off my land."

Kerrigan spread his arms in a helpless gesture. "Why, certainly, Captain. At once, now." He backed off the porch and Roarity followed. They waited in the street under a cottonwood, the rain sifting through its branches.

Kerrigan smiled. "Missed the bull, got the calf."

"I don't like it."

"Ah, it's for the best, surely. The old man will keep his gob shut with his boy in the thick of it."

Roarity shrugged and looked away from the house.

🍀

Inside, Niall was hurriedly throwing his clothes into a sack. There were few things he had—a change of clothing, one decent suit, pocketknife, a rosary made of string—boy's things.

Sean, who shared the room with him, was bewildered. "Why are you goin', Niall? Why?"

"I can't explain, Sean. I just have to."

"You have a fight with Pa?"

Niall shook his head. "Not really." He remembered in an intuitive instant the many kindnesses of his father and he recalled the struggles, the sacrifices, the acts of quiet courage. "I've no quarrel with Pa, Sean. Like as not he's right this time as always. But I feel . . ." He stopped. "I don't know what I feel. But don't go blamin' Pa. Mind him, you hear. There's no man like him in all the hills."

Sean's eyes clouded up so that Niall added, "And don't you be worryin'. Sure, I'll see you often. Not here, but somewheres."

Sean lunged at his brother, clung to him. "I don't want you to go, Niall. I want to go with you." He began to cry.

"Now, none of that. I said I'd see you and I mean it. Besides, it was too crowded here. Now you'll have the whole room to yourself."

"I don't want the room. I want you, Niall."

Near tears himself, Niall pulled away from his brother. "Good-bye, Sean. And don't blame Pa."

He walked through the kitchen where Kitty was crying in Jimmy's arms and her embarrassed suitor stared stupidly, without comment. Bridget stopped Niall by the door.

"You go now, Niall, and your father'll not let you back. You know he means it?"

"Yes, Ma, I know," Niall said wearily. "Can't you understand either?"

"I try to understand, Niall. God knows I do. But all I can see is my boy leavin' and the family never again the same."

Niall choked back the tears. "I'm not goin' to the end of the world, Ma. Just a few miles from here. Somewhere I can get a place. You'll see me. And maybe Pa will change." He made this last statement without believing it.

Bridget shook her head. "No, Niall, it won't be the same ever again. It's the family breakin' up and an angry day for us all. Don't shame your Pa or me, you hear. And God bless you."

They both reached out to embrace one another and awkwardly feinted for position, ending with a clumsy clasp. That was the last thing Niall remembered—that awkward farewell.

When Bridget heard the door slam, she knew he had gone with Kerrigan and Roarity. From behind the ragged curtain in his room, Mike watched the trio disappear down the road. He let the curtain drop and sagged back on his bed, pressing one grizzled fist into the opposite palm.

The rains pounded down, cracking at the slate roof, blurring the window panes, sweeping over the mass grave in Pottsville, and hurtling down the road after Niall. He turned his collar against it and never looked back.

THREE

The Long Strike

Captain Mike was right about one thing—within weeks there was bloodshed.

At first the feuds were local and limited. Take, for example, the hostilities that erupted in Mahanoy City when two rival volunteer fire companies met at the scene of a small blaze and utilized the occasion to square off against each other, Irishman versus Englishman. Scattered fist fights merged into a general melee, the melee became a riot, and the riot terminated in reckless shooting. George Major, chief burgess of Mahanoy City, was killed. Arrested and accused of the murder was Dan Dougherty, himself seriously wounded in the affray. Dougherty's trial drew widespread attention and feelings were both rabid and biased. In the face of much adverse testimony, Dougherty consented to a desperation measure and submitted himself to a dangerous operation to remove the bullet lodged in his body. When extracted, the bullet proved to have come from Major's pistol and Dougherty was freed. The acquittal merely intensified the hatred on both sides and set the stage for open conflict.

Since Major's death, small skirmishes had been occurring throughout the coalfields. Now they were building toward an all-out war. In late spring, the miners dropped their tools and left the pits.

Behind them was the experience of failure in previous strikes, but the miners were determined upon this final effort. They settled down to a long siege. All expected the suffering to be extreme but they had endured hardships for less cause. Generally, their participation was spontaneous. Some men— like Mike and Jimmy Boyle—stayed away from the mines because work had stopped. Most of the men shared the militant spirit of Niall Flannery and became active demonstrators. No support came from the Miners' National Association. In fact, their action was criticized and, even on the local level, there was much dissension. Despite divided leadership, terrible odds, and stark poverty, the miners persevered, exhibiting an iron discipline and a marvelous spirit of sacrifice. At stake were a more stable wage scale (one comparable to that of the previous year), enforcement of the safety inspection laws, a shorter work week, less company control, and some other secondary conditions.

Equally determined were the mine owners. For years they had feared the unions and they saw in the defeat of this strike a chance to deal them a crushing blow. So they organized into the Anthracite Board of Trade and accepted Franklin B. Gowen of the Philadelphia and Reading Railroad as their general. New recruits were fed into the Coal and Iron Police until they formed a small private army. To keep track of plans and to spot labor leaders, Pinkerton detectives were hired to infiltrate mine unions as spies.

From the beginning, the owners agreed there would be

no concessions. In the risky enterprise they conducted, they did not want to add the final imponderable of split jurisdiction. With their vast resources of wealth and with the power of the state behind them, they could afford to wait out their opponents. Even when the miners later backed down on some of their wage demands and merely asked for a voice in the settlement of coal rates, the companies refused to negotiate.

So the miners marched. The heavy tread of thousands of feet echoed through the valley. Sometimes the march was deliberately staged. Sometimes it was improvised as a group assembled near a colliery, the town hall, or an isolated patch in the hills. From here they would sally forth, calling upon any miners still employed to come out and join them. As the men tumbled out of the shafts to enlist in the parade, the miners would tramp on—from city to city, from colliery to colliery. Thousands of them were on the road in a brazen show of defiance. Often, as they marched, they would sing extemporaneous tunes.

Now two months are over—that no one can deny,
And for to stand another, we are willing for to try.
Our wages will not be reduced, tho' poverty do reign.
We'll have the seventy-four basis, boys, before we work
again.

Then there were the times when the singing stopped. Heard instead were the sounds of gunfire and crackling timber and human agony.

At Tamaqua, the telegraph office was burned and incendiaries destroyed mine shafts and out buildings at Coal Castle and Irontown. The breaker at Mahanoy City was fired, rebuilt, and fired again within the month.

Every train that moved coal was in danger. Crews were stoned by miners haunting the roadbeds. Coal cars were dumped; trains derailed. Occasionally a group of miners would swarm aboard the cars and smash them to useless fragments.

The miners marched on—Mauch Chunk, Wilkes-Barre, Lebanon, Luzerne. Destruction followed in their wake. Mine officials, watchmen, and police were waylaid and beaten. Bullets cracked and whistled in the dark streets. Robberies were frequent with every conceivable type of item disappearing—money, tools, food, clothing, dynamite, even mules.

Nor were the operators idle. While there were few open battles, the Coal and Iron Police, better armed and organized, dropped attacking miners with their clubs or rifle fire. And the police, teaming with sympathetic vigilantes known as "sheet iron gangs," carried out raids of their own, sweeping into a mining patch, beating and shooting householders and burning their dwellings.

Night was the time of terror. In Pottsville they established "deadlines," such as those found in lawless frontier towns, and citizens of both camps dared not cross this arbitrary limit after dark. Ambush was a commonplace and assault a regular occurrence. The death toll mounted.

Taggart was jumped one evening by three masked men. He fought back savagely but was soundly thrashed and hospitalized for a week. When he recovered he replied in kind. The local police contingent was doubled and sent to prowl on unwary miners, beating them into unconsciousness.

Posted everywhere were the miners' "pistol notices," warning their enemies of dire consequences to follow. Crudely lettered and composed, they were often accompanied by sketches of pistols or daggers or coffins or the hangman's noose. McDonald received such a threat in June and read it with trembling hands.

> Mister crooked storekeeper, if you don't leave in two days time you will meat your doom. their will Bee a open war. imeateatly. Bee carefull the above don't Bee your home in a short time.

There was a drawing of an open grave in the corner. McDonald read the note twice, shuddered, and read it again. He folded it gingerly into a shirt pocket and then thoughtfully cracked his knuckles. The next day he pulled out of Pottsville, whipping his mangy mule team down the dusty road that ended at Philadelphia. Every time he picked up a newspaper for months afterward, he congratulated himself on his escape. It took Bridget only two visits to the company store to transfer her intense dislike to his successor.

On the Fourth of July, 1875, there were no celebrations— unless you count the riot at the Buckville Colliery and six separate fires at the Number Five hole in Panther Creek Valley. Most of the miners squatted at home, grim and hungry, or they gathered in small knots around the vacant mines, as if the black mood could destroy the cause of their anger.

Captain Mike hunkered uncomfortably on his hot porch. On his lap was his dog-eared Bible but his eyes fell upon no comforting words. Instead they looked blankly into space revealing doubt and indecision.

In the cramped yard knelt Sean, watching a toad prey on

an anthill. The air hung heavily over the patch. For weeks the sun had burned the grass dry and no breeze disturbed the brown blades. Where there was no grass, there was coal dust; and where there was no dust, the earth cracked in ragged seams. Sean was placid, favoring the ants, but allowing nature to pursue its relentless pattern.

Mike, too, was pensive, the sweat coursing down his face and his palms wet against the Bible's leather binding. Bridget's step disturbed him.

"Mike, love, I'd like a word with ye."

He gestured for her to sit beside him but she declined.

"It's but a short speech I'll make, and it's no surprise, I'm sure. But the sad fact is we've about reached bottom in the Flannery larder and there's hardly a place will give me credit. That's the long and short of it."

Mike nodded. "It's been hard, I know. For everyone."

Bridget shrugged her shoulders. "It's not for complainin' I come but for to find answers. There's the four of us needin' grub and I can't be fetchin' it like the Lord in your Bible makin' loaves and fishes."

Mike knew she was after the money he had saved and he knew she was right in demanding it. Perhaps there might be another chance at the farm. In his heart he had abandoned the hope but dreams die hard when dreaming is difficult. Still, the family had to eat. Already there were those who had slaughtered their mules, their dogs, and their cats. Squirrels and rabbits were no longer hunted in sport but fiercely, by desperate men with empty stomachs. Birds were snared and cooked and, in some cases, grass was eaten to stave off death. Many succumbed—young and old—and it was the famine all over again. Every town and village echoed to the sound of coffins being constructed. Emaciated families, each member a walking skeleton, staggered out of the valley, hoping for something better on the other side of the mountain. Their ragged bodies were often found along the road, faces in the dust or looking up, hollow-eyed, into the merciless sun.

Mike thought of all these things and he knew he must act. A good officer always kept a reserve and now he must part with his. "Sean," he called, postponing the decision, "why is it you've not been fishin' these many days? A good trout would make a mighty fine meal. Not lost your taste for it, have you?"

"It ain't the same, Pa, not havin' Niall along. Just haven't felt like it." The words were out before Sean thought about them.

"Aye." Captain Mike nodded, then he sighed and instructed Bridget. "There's money I kept back against a move someday, Bridget. It's in the tin box next to my tools. But likely you knew that already."

Bridget smiled mischievously. "Sure, I'd be a poor housewife if I didn't. Shall I fetch it?"

"Do that like the good girl. I expect our first move is to stay alive before we think of farms and such. Bring it to me and we'll eat for a while yet." He pulled his pipe from his pocket and sucked reflectively on the dry stem. Then he closed the Bible and sat back.

In the yard the toad was both satisfied and bored. He hopped sluggishly into the weeds. Sean arose, shuffled up on the porch, and sat beside his father.

"Pa, do you think it'll be much longer? The strike, I mean."

Mike answered the question indifferently, as if it had been

posed by a newspaper reporter. "I think not, although there's a great deal of fire on both sides yet."

"Sometimes I even miss the breaker, Pa. I think of all the coal sittin' down below and the cars rustin' and all. It don't seem right."

Captain Mike turned the pipe stem slowly in his fingers. He looked down at Sean. "Well, lad, you know my views. I'd be workin' there now if they'd let me. But there's other good men feel different and they're entitled to their opinions, I expect. Mining's a hard enough life. Dirt and heat and dampness and achin' limbs all day. Then too tired at night to even play with the children. You know, Sean, I don't believe we've ever been fishin', just the two of us."

"No, Pa, we ain't."

Mike made a sudden resolution. "Well, there's nothing stoppin' us now. You get your pole and tell your Ma. Where's the best place?"

Sean was on his feet, excited and happy for the first time in weeks. "Turner's Creek is tops, Pa, for trout. Only about three miles from here I know a place. Me and Nia—ah—me and some of the other boys—ah—we go there a lot."

"Get along, then, and tell your Ma."

They fished all afternoon and caught three trout and a few shiners. The brook was running clear and cool and the interlocking branches shielded them from the day's heat. And Sean heard his father laugh—a strange and welcome experience. Coming home, his father laughed again and put his arm around the boy's shoulder.

"Good man. Those fish will fry up like a mine owner's supper."

It made the strike seem distant and unreal. But, two nights

later, there was another killing in Tamaqua. The inquest fixed the time at 2:30 A.M. on the morning of July 6.

Barney McCarron, frightened by recent happenings, requested Benjamin J. Yost, a fellow policeman, to accompany him on his rounds to extinguish the city's lights. They paced silently and nervously through the night, Barney with the short ladder and Yost swinging the long snuffing stick in his big right hand. The town slumbered uneasily, with hunger unfulfilled and violence at the edge of every dream.

Yost was a large-featured man, tall and broad through the shoulders. He spoke with a heavy German accent. "You remember last night, Barney, when we walk by the saloon? Them three fellers was from the other side, across Summit Hill. I think they want trouble with us."

"Not while there's the two of us. You've mixed with the same types enough in the past and it's them always lands in the jailhouse."

Yost nodded, then shook his head. "But my wife—she worries all the time. I be glad when the mines they are open again. Not so much trouble for us."

They had reached the corner of Broad and Lehigh Streets and Barney McCarron, puffing slightly, set the ladder up against the gaslight pole. "I hope you're right, Ben, about the trouble stoppin' when the miners go back. I'll wager things'll never quiet. When both sides wants money and only one a them got it, watch out."

It was very still. You could hear the river faintly gurgling and the sawing sound of the crickets. Even the squeak of the lamp door being opened echoed in the gloom. Three men heard it as they crouched behind the wall of the town's old cemetery, not a hundred yards away. Stealthily, two of them left the hiding place and descended into the street.

"Last one," said Yost. "Then we go home. My old woman is waiting up for me. Can you see the light there? You come with and we have coffee."

"I will, though a cold glass would go better. It's past two in the morning and already as hot as noon."

Yost ascended the ladder and reached up for the flickering flame. Neither he nor Barney saw the figures emerge from the darkness. The first shot caught Yost in the side and he tumbled drunkenly into the street. Barney McCarron dashed for cover. The firing persisted, erratic and harmless. Then, as lights began to prick the black night, the gunmen faded back to the cemetery, joined their waiting companion, and fled through the hills.

Mrs. Yost had raced into the street at the first report, screaming in anticipation of what she would find. She knelt by her husband, moaning. Two neighbor women, with shawls thrown hastily over their nightgowns, were beside her in a few minutes to comfort her. When the doctor arrived, Yost was still conscious.

"Carry him to his house," the doctor ordered. Three men lifted him, still bleeding badly, and bore him to his small frame home. Here they laid him on his couch where the doctor ripped off his shirt and began bathing the wound. Mrs. Yost continued to kneel by her husband, stroking his hands and sobbing incoherently.

"Did you see them?" a man inquired of Mrs. Yost.

"No. Only the flash of the guns. Only the noise. I knew it would be him. I told him." She repeated her wailing.

Yost opened his eyes and the doctor asked, "How does it feel?"

The policeman shook his head slowly. "I will die."

Barney McCarron had stolen in, sheepishly. He crept to the deathbed and heard Yost's final statement.

"There was two of them. They come down from the graveyard. Two Irishmen. I think they was after Barney. I think they was. That's why I go with him to outen the lights. They make mistake and shoot me, I think. Barney was afraid of them. We see them last night at the saloon, I bet, the same ones. I point them out to Barney. Two fellers from the other side. Two Irishmen."

Those were the last words he spoke.

By sunup, the police were searching for the killers, roaming the hills and questioning all the settlers in the neighboring patches. Rumor soon had Powder Keg Kerrigan as one of the assailants but, when arrested and interrogated, he vehemently denied everything. They did not hold him but placed him under surveillance. Among his friends, Kerrigan laughed and boasted that he had done the shooting. The police waited.

When Sunday came, it was a day of uneasy truce. Somewhere in the churchgoing crowds, perhaps, lurked the murderers of Yost. With them were others who had killed and robbed and burned. These men stood, too, when the priest entered and they heard the same Kyrie and the same Gospel. Like all of the others seeking solace in the Mass, they settled back for the words of Father McDermott.

"In today's Gospel," said the priest, "we hear the words of Christ warning us against false prophets and telling us that by their fruits we shall know them. Because, as the Lord tells us, 'every good tree bears good fruit but the bad tree bears bad fruit.' Like all the parables of Christ, there is meaning in this, not only for the Jews of old, but for us today—here, in Pottsville."

He cleared his throat and shifted a little in the rough pine pulpit.

"This is a time of serious trouble for us all. Every family has had some sorrow, some bereavement. But there has been sin mixed with the sorrow. And these trials may be punishment for the evil we have done. For all of us, dear people, have contributed to this evil. Should I keep silent about this? I would not be your priest if I did so.

"I tell you nothing but the truth when I say that we have few friends among the mine bosses and operators. Most of them are anti-Catholic or anti-Irish or both. We know these things to be true. We know that some of them have quietly killed our fellow workers or have driven them from this region to become hewers of wood or drawers of water for others.

"But this evil thing has overcome many of us. We have become as bad as those who persecute us. In the name of freedom, some men have taken lives and destroyed property. Revenge has led others to kill. There is nothing in this but sin. And the sinner, we know, shall be punished. By the fruits shall you know them. Sin answers nothing. Sin defeats everything.

"When you are deep in the mine—so deep that the air is thin and the water seeps around your ankles—who is with you? And suppose you are alone or lost in a blank corridor— who knows you are there? God knows. He knows your every act from rising to nightfall, from sleeping to waking. He is with you in your hunger, in the blackness of the pit, in the depths of your souls. Do not think to fool Him with blasphemous oaths and secret societies. He knows who are the members. He knows whose hands have spilled blood. 'Vengeance is mine,' says the Lord.

"The Church has always taught the evil of secret societies, joined for immoral purposes. Do not be misled by these ravenous wolves, as the Bible tells us, but shun them as you would the rotten fruit. For, like the fruit, they will fall and be burned.

"I tell you these things, not to destroy hope, but to preserve charity. When the cause for anger is great, the cause for love is greater. You must love those who hate you. And you must pray for them."

There was a stir in the back of the little frame church. Jake Roarity lurched to his feet and shouted, "I'll see them in hell. They're the thieves and the murderers and ourselves the victims. Had you eyes to see that, Father McDermott, there'd be no need of sermons." He wheeled and was out the door in a moment.

The congregation sat stunned. No one ever spoke back to the priest on the altar. The very thought was sacrilegious. Yet Jake Roarity had done so. Pious women crossed themselves as if some unseen spirit hovered near them. Captain Mike hung his head, embarrassed for Father McDermott. But there were some mutterings of approval and some who praised inwardly the courage of Roarity. They figured the Church had no cause to criticize the Mollies. Not publicly, at least.

Father McDermott looked over the heads of the congregation at the open door. There were tears of anger and frustration in his eyes. Not only his sacred office but also his New England background asserted itself. The act was both profane and impolite. He looked back at his notes but could not continue. "Amen," he said and blessed them absently. Then he heaved his tiny shoulders in a massive sigh and returned to the altar.

"Credo in unum Deo," he said aloud. I believe in one God. .. who for us men and our salvation came down from heaven. "For Roarity, too," he interpolated silently. "For all men." He arched his back to kiss the altar.

When the Mass concluded, the people streamed out, buzzing about the unusual incident. Kitty was particularly shocked, as she confided to Jimmy Boyle. "Sure, and I thought the Lord would strike him then and there. It was like the devil himself risin' up and blasphemin'."

Jimmy laughed. "Roarity's no Beelzebub, that's certain. Just a rash man is all and pretty much fired up. Did you not hear one of his children sickened and died this week past? Partly daft, I suppose he is, and a strong-tempered man even in normal times."

"I didn't know about the child. Still—"

"Still there's no cause for it, I know." Jimmy lapsed into silence and Kitty respected his mood, only stealing a look at his sober profile as they continued along the path.

"Jimmy, have you marched with the men at all?"

"Sometimes."

"You've not been with them when ... ?" She couldn't phrase the question.

Jimmy shook his head. "I've been in no scrapes if that's what you mean. A little marchin' and a little singin' and not a bit of anything else. Might be I haven't the courage for the real fight."

"That's not true." After a pause Kitty asked, "What about the Mollies?"

Jimmy shook his head again. "I've had no truck with them."

"Good, then, for they're all bad men like Father says."

"I'm not so sure of that. Sure, your own brother is said to be one of them."

"Niall wouldn't."

Jimmy shrugged. "They're not demons, you know, Kitty, but only men. And some of them is common men with a common cause who would as soon be home in their beds did they not feel as they do."

"I can't see it." Kitty shook her dark curls in denial.

At that moment, Brendan came abreast of them and swung an arm around each pair of shoulders. "By your looks, this is serious talk," he teased, "and not befittin' them as is to be married."

Jimmy's face broke into a boyish grin while Kitty flushed and turned away.

"Well, then, there is to be a weddin', isn't there? Or has the strike wrung all the love out of young folks? I'd call it a good trainin' time, for there'll be trouble enough after you're married."

"There's no date been set, Brendan," Kitty explained softly.

The old man nodded. "What you young folks need, I do believe, is an old Irish matchmaker to make all the arrangements."

"No, thank you," said Kitty archly. "I'd not like bein' discussed and bargained for like a piece of merchandise."

Brendan winked at Jimmy. "Ah, now, it's not such a bad system. Makes more sense than half the weddin's these days."

Jimmy laughed. "It'll be next year, perhaps, if things quiet some."

Lifting a stunted forefinger in playful warning, Brendan

counseled them. "There's many things that wait. One's a mother for her son, or a dog for its master, a fish for the hook, maybe, and coal for the miner's pick. But love doesn't wait in the young. I'd think about it." He dropped the finger, patted Kitty and Jimmy on the shoulders, and strolled off.

Not far from the church, Niall waited. As his parents approached, he stepped from behind a rickety porch and confronted his father.

"Pa, I want to explain about Yost. I had nothin' to do with it. Nor with any of the other killin's."

Mike paused, cloaking his emotion at the welcome confession. When he spoke it was with restraint. "But you sleep and eat with those who kill. You've the same blood on your hands. You're in league with them."

Niall bit his lip in exasperation. "Pa, you never try to understand. You're blind to all faults but those of your own kind. We *have* to win. Otherwise all of this will have been in vain."

Mike turned away. "Come along, Bridget. We're late and there could be weather brewin'." Not an angry cloud could be seen, so Niall understood the rebuff.

Bridget held her husband by the arm. "Mike."

"Come along." He walked away from her. She turned to Niall, kissed him on the cheek, and held his troubled face in her hands for an instant. Then she ran after Mike.

Sean had lagged behind the others. "Hello, Niall." Niall was still watching his parents but he turned around slowly and looked down at his brother. Smiling, he ran his hand through Sean's hair.

"How's the big room without me?"

"I wish you were home."

"So do I, Sean. Maybe soon. I believe we've a chance for

what we're after. There's no coal been taken out of the mines for months. That means no profits for the owners. They'll give in."

"Pa says it's us will give in when there's no more food at all."

"That's Pa, all right. But how have you been? Are you and Kitty and the folks making out for food and all?"

"Oh, yes. But you? You're thinner, Niall."

"Well, there's no excuse for bein' fat. A few days with a pick and a few good meals and I'll be right as ever."

Sean leaned against the porch and said, reflectively, "I wish I was goin' down in the pit with you and Pa when you go. Niall, I never been down—not even to see."

"There's nothing much to see, Sean." Niall's eyes narrowed and his tone was bitter. "Nothin' except men coughin' and sweatin' and near naked in the heat. Nothin' but the damp smell and the sound of picks and fallin' coal and the wagons always creakin' for the next lot. You'll be there soon enough. Don't wish it on yourself." He broke the mood with a smile.

"Best I be goin', Niall. Maybe we can go fishin' some day. Pa took me once."

"Good. Some day, maybe in a week or so. I could meet you at Turner's Creek. Fair enough?"

"Fair enough." Sean dashed after his parents.

Niall watched them go. He'd have liked to run after them, to beg forgiveness of his father and embrace his mother. It would be good to sleep in his old room and waken to the smell of food. It would be good to be home. He turned away and paced slowly toward Carroll's Saloon.

James Carroll was an unlikely looking tavern owner. His

features were those of a poet, with feminine hands and ta-pered fingers. His person was neat and his clothes a cut above the miners' best. Nothing seemed to escape his deep-set eyes but he said very little. He had a full head of dark hair, a thin mustache which he kept carefully trimmed, and a sharp chin that was often propped on his chest in an attitude of repose. His wife and four children lived a lonely existence at the local hotel while he brooded over his customers and over working conditions. Although he sympathized with the min-ers, he never took sides openly, for business was business. In all, he was a simple, introspective, unspectacular man but his saloon was being watched because dangerous men gathered here. If he was aware of this, he did not show it. When Niall walked in, he scarcely nodded but continued polishing the bar glasses.

Although this was the gathering place for the idle min-ers, the Sunday afternoon crowd was small. It would liven up after dark. Then there would be a flare of tempers and fre-quent fights and James Carroll would have to intervene and keep order.

Niall spotted Kerrigan and Roarity seated at one of the circular tables. They were in animated conversation with Thomas Duffy, a young engineer from the Buckville Colliery, and husky Hugh McGehan. All were drinking save McGehan, a total abstainer from alcohol and a man inordinately proud of his fine physique. McGehan was 21, illiterate, and quick-tempered. This latter quality got him blacklisted two weeks before the strike started. Duffy was more sociable, more intel-ligent, but he enjoyed the adventuresome spirit generated by this infamous company. Kerrigan signaled for Niall to join them.

Niall swung a chair from a nearby table and slid into it, scowling at Roarity. "Nice scene you pulled today."

Roarity colored and looked around angrily. "Let him watch his own tongue. You're all ridden by the priests. You, Niall, as well as the rest. But not Jake Roarity. I've no ears to hear when they preach against the workin' man."

"Why go to church, then?"

Roarity shrugged. "Habit, I guess. But it can be broken."

Niall grunted contemptuously. "You'd do better to keep that habit and lose some of your others."

"What's ailin' you?" Roarity tilted his chair back and regarded Niall quizzically.

"Nothin'."

Kerrigan spoke up now, sarcastically. "Like to go home, would you, Niall?" His bulky head rested on his fists and there was a sly smile prompting him.

Niall glared at him. "I'm in this the same as you, you know that."

Kerrigan shook his head. "I don't know it, for one. All you've done is march with us and drink with us and jabber with us. When the fightin' come to be done, you was always somewheres else."

"Like the killin' of Yost, you mean? That's the sort of fightin' suits you, Kerrigan. Sneakin' in the dark and firin' from the safety of the shadows."

Kerrigan stood up, fists clenched, and Niall jumped up to face him. Carroll stopped polishing the glasses and watched. But Roarity slammed the table with his hand. "Sit down! Both of you!"

The tension was broken and, slowly, they obeyed.

"Look, Niall, none of this about the Yost thing. Maybe Powder Keg did it and maybe he didn't. Don't forget there was two men done the shootin' and maybe someone waitin' nearby. Coulda been me or McGehan here." Roarity paused and let the next statement sink in. "Coulda been you, Niall."

"I was nowheres near there."

Roarity shrugged. "Your word against the others maybe." He paused again and became more friendly. "But there's no need of fightin' among ourselves. Kerrigan's right about your not comin' along with us. Why, you ain't even been swore into the society."

"I don't want swearin' in."

"The priest botherin' you?"

"Maybe. Maybe I just don't like the idea myself."

"All right. But how about the other? Will you march with us next time or do you want to sit back and let other men do your fightin' for you?"

Niall frowned, then looked away. "I'll go."

"Tonight?"

"Tonight." Niall still avoided looking at his companions. This brought a smile to Roarity's crabbed face. "You won't have to walk far then, lad, for we're firin' Number Nine—your own colliery right here in Pottsville."

Niall looked up quickly, darted a glance at the leering, expectant faces. Then he stared straight at Roarity. "I said I'd go."

FOUR

Niall

Oliver Taggart's cabin squatted at the end of the road, nearest the colliery. As a result of this location, it was the dingiest dwelling within the town. And its interior matched the exterior. Only the most elementary household chores were performed by the mine boss. Coal dust, food particles, and scraps of paper were everywhere. The place lacked the touch which a woman had once given it.

Tonight Taggart dined alone as usual, wolfing down the last of his stew and then swallowing a big mouthful of coffee. Setting down the mug, he gripped it with both hands, liking the sturdy feel of it. His elbows leaned on a table slick with grease. Somehow, though, he kept himself clean amid this welter of filth. Perhaps this was because he was seldom home, pausing here only to sleep and eat.

There was a sharp knock on his door. He wiped his mouth with his hand. Another knock.

"Come in," he bellowed. "Don't knock down the door."

The door swung open, revealing a frightened little man who darted inside and closed the door behind him.

"Well, man, what is it?"

"The name's Silk, Mr. Taggart. Matt Silk. I'm ticket boss on the weighing crew." The stranger smiled hesitantly, exposing a ragged set of yellow teeth. "I'm tellin' you this so's you might remember me kindly for bringin' you the news."

Taggart stood up, impatiently. "What news? Out with it."

"There'll be an attempt on the colliery tonight." Silk's little animal eyes watched the effect on Taggart.

"Where'd you hear this?"

"It's gospel. I heard it in Carroll's place."

Taggart nodded, his mind racing. "What time and who's to be in on it?"

"Can't say about that, Mr. Taggart." Silk's hands fluttered in a timid gesture of ignorance.

Taggart stepped to him and seized him by the throat. "You're a liar. You know who was doin' the talkin'. Out with it or I'll tear your head off!"

Silk gasped, his eyes protruding. "No, Mr. Taggart. The Mollies will get me sure if I tell. I only wanted you to know about the plan. That's all."

Taggart tightened his grip on the man's throat. "Come on!"

"No—please!"

"There'll be nothin' left for the Molly Maguires after I get through with you. Last chance!" He applied more pressure. Silk struggled, his fingers scraping the bulging knuckles of Taggart and terror written in his staring eyes. He nodded and Taggart released him. For a few seconds he merely groaned and rubbed his red neck.

Taggart snapped his fingers. "Let's have it."

"Kerrigan was there. And Roarity. And Niall Flannery."

"The Captain's boy?"

Silk nodded. "McGehan, too, and Duffy. Maybe some others but I don't know."

"How about the time?"

"I swear I don't know. They never said. I swear."

Taggart nodded, then waved his hand in dismissal. "I'll try to remember this, Silk. Now you remember to keep quiet about it to anyone else."

"Yes, sir; yes, sir." Silk hurried away, still massaging his throat.

Leaving his coffee unfinished, Taggart moved to the corner of his kitchen where his Winchester was propped. He loaded it and thrust some extra shells into his pocket. Then he stepped into the street, now laced by twilight shadows. Swiftly, he moved to the colliery. Inside the watchman's shack he found a guard eating the remnants of his supper.

"I'll stick here," Taggart informed him. "You head out to the sergeant's house. Tell him to get here on the double with all the men he can find. And tell him to do it quietly, you hear?"

The guard nodded.

"Then get going."

Taggart permitted himself a satisfied smile as he walked outside the shack seeking a good firing point. The road from town rose gradually, cresting just below the mine shaft. This hill was part earth, part coal, and sloped slightly for two hundred yards. Near the top, Taggart found a cluster of logs and rain barrels which formed a small fortress. He dragged some of them together, rolling a log toward the front and then stretching out behind it. Again he checked his rifle and practiced sighting on various points along the road.

There were stars out and a thin crescent moon which

shed little light. From town, Taggart could hear sounds of drunken revelry mingled with mothers calling children in from play. The mine was strangely still, its machinery inert and its wooden tower like a ghostly citadel. Taggart pulled his watch from his pocket and squinted at it. His men should be back in fifteen minutes, maybe twenty. He lay on his stomach and waited.

From the gloom a new sound reached him—muffled voices. His men or the Mollies? Taggart steadied his Winchester. A few shapes began to emerge below the hill, then more. There must be a dozen men. Whispers became audible as the approaching men scattered, signaling to one another, and then fanning out and creeping forward stealthily.

"It's them," Taggart said to himself. "Blast it! Where's that sergeant?"

Suddenly a match was struck below and a torch leaped into flame, illumining the features of one attacker.

"Kerrigan," Taggart whispered to himself.

Another man stalked beside Kerrigan and the remaining men in the wide semicircle jumped up and started running toward the shaft. Chunks of coal rumbled down as they scrambled up the slope.

Taggart waited until they were less than fifty yards away. Then he fired, missing Kerrigan but striking his companion. The line of charging men halted, undecided, and then dropped to the ground. Kerrigan hurled his torch at the shed but it fell short. Taggart fired again and, this time, his fire was returned. Where were the police? The window behind him shattered as a bullet struck and he heard several more chunk into his barricade. His palms were sweating as he fired again into the night. He could see the crouching forms slithering forward, hear their feet grinding on the slate. A bullet whined by his ear and he fired wildly down the hillside.

Just when it seemed they might rush him, he heard shouts from the road. Roarity heard them, too, and shouted a warning. "Blacklegs! Fall back!" The miners jumped up and raced down the mound, tumbling in their anxiety to escape.

Taggart sent an ineffectual volley after them and a few of the police discharged their weapons aimlessly into the darkness. At the door of the watchman's shed, Taggart met them, angrily. "You took your sweet time."

The sergeant apologized. "We come as fast as we could. Looks like no harm done. You see any of them?"

"Hit one, I think. Let's take a look."

The police, led by the mine boss, filed down the hill until they reached the bottom.

"Over here, sir!" called one of the guards.

Taggart trotted over to the waiting policeman. At his feet was the blackened body of a man. It had rolled all the way down the hillside, churning through the dust.

"Bring a light!" Taggart turned the man over with his boot and thrust a match in his face. For a moment he studied the dead man's features, then he blew out the match.

"You know him?" asked the sergeant.

"Niall Flannery."

"Dead?"

"Caught it chest high. Dead before he rolled this far, I'd say."

The sergeant shuddered involuntarily. "Poor devil." Then he recovered. "Not that he didn't deserve it. But I mean, out here, covered with coal and all."

Taggart cradled his rifle in his arms and started up the hill. He turned to the sergeant. "Have someone take word to his folks in West Patch. Just have them ask for Captain Mike." He paused. "Tell him where he can find his boy." Frowning in the darkness, he repeated. "Tell him where he can find his boy." He clambered slowly back toward the shed.

"Yes, sir."

The sergeant did not like the assignment, but four men were dispatched and they made their way warily through Pottsville and across the hill that separated the town from the mining patch. On the outskirts they encountered Brendan of Ballycotton.

"Which way to Flannery's shack?" The leader hoped his gruffness would hide his fear.

Brendan shrugged. "Sure, I'm a stranger meself. I wouldn't be knowin' the man. Flannery, you say?"

"Aye, Flannery. But it's not what you may think. There's been some shootin' and his boy's got shot up."

"Niall, is it?" Brendan forgot his cloak of ignorance.

"You said you didn't know the Flannerys."

"Is it Niall?"

"Aye."

"Dead?"

"As a lump of slag."

Brendan lowered his head and folded his hands. "God have mercy." He stood there, ignoring the police, and shaking his white head. "Niall."

"Come on, old man. Where's the house?"

"I'll go meself. Where's the boy?"

"At the foot of the colliery, next to the road."

Brendan shuffled off and the quartet of police turned their

backs on him and walked rapidly out of the patch. Brendan continued to Captain Mike's place, halted, and then walked to the door and rapped.

Bridget started up, exchanged glances with Mike and then sat down. Sean moved to unbar the door but his father checked him.

"Hold a minute, Sean." Mike strode to the door himself. "Who's there?"

"Sure, it's only Brendan."

Mike let him in, apologizing. "So much goin' on these nights, a man can't be too careful."

Brendan nodded. He couldn't take his eyes off Bridget. And he couldn't get out the words he'd come to say.

"Well, is there somethin' you come for, Brendan?"

The old man sighed. "There is, Mike. On the road back there I come across some blacklegs. Four a them. They was lookin' for your house."

Bridget stood, wide-eyed, and moved toward him. "It's about Niall, isn't it?" She fairly screamed,

"It is. There's been a shootin' near the colliery and he was hit. He's—there now."

"Come on!" Mike darted for the door. Brendan halted him. "Mike, the boy's dead." Stunned, Mike relaxed his grip on the latch. His shoulders sagged. In his eyes, tears formed quickly and a sudden stabbing pain struck his throat. He sat in a chair and dropped his head in his hands. Bridget was sobbing and murmuring, "Dear God, dear God." Sean tried vainly to comfort her, his own eyes wet.

"How did it happen?" Mike asked it without looking up from his hands.

"An attempt to fire the mine, Mike. Heard it was comin' meself but never thought of Niall bein' with them. Must have been spotted before they got the job done."

Jimmy Boyle ran in, Kitty at his heels. "Mr. Flannery, we met some police on the road and they . . ." He stopped, realizing the news had preceded him. Kitty clung to her mother, both weeping hysterically. "It was Taggart done the shootin'," Jimmy added weakly.

Mike looked up but there was no anger in his eyes, only confusion. "Come on," he said finally. "Let's go get him."

Sean, Jimmy, and Brendan followed him. Bridget gasped. "Mike, not Sean."

"It's his brother, Bridget. Besides, we'll need him." Half-running, half-walking, they came into Pottsville. A curious crowd marked the spot near the colliery where Niall lay. Mike pushed his way through them. For a long moment, he looked down on his son, then knelt beside him and held his face in his hands. Staring into those unseeing eyes, he just shook his head and wept. Sean was beside him, blubbering fitfully, and wiping off his brother's grimy face with his own kerchief.

With a great effort, Mike controlled himself, kissed Niall on the forehead, and turned to his companions. "Let's carry him home."

As Brendan reached down for Niall, a thought struck him and he voiced it aloud. "And no priest with him at the end."

"Please God, and he didn't need one."

Sean grabbed his brother's leg as they hoisted him to a carrying position. Still sobbing, he caressed the lifeless limb as if he could rub life back into it. There would be no more walks together. And no fishing at Turner's Creek.

The crowd parted and let them through, following them a few hundred yards until the road turned to West Patch. Then they dispersed, leaving the family and friends to attend to Niall's homecoming.

FIVE

The Red-headed
Stranger

*B*ridget and Kitty wore black for two months, until September came and leaves drifted through the valley and across the crude mound which covered Niall Flannery. There were other new graves there for those who had died from violence, from hunger, from illness. Wooden crosses poked grimly from the fresh earth.

Contrary to the opinions of many of his friends, Captain Mike took no action against Taggart nor the mine owners.

"If anyone's to blame, it's meself," he confided to Brendan one day, weeks after the funeral. "Meself and Niall. He was warned and I should have seen to it. There's no fault in the others."

"Roarity was sayin' ..."

"Don't speak that name!" Mike softened his voice. "I've avoided the man, him and Kerrigan. I'd as soon not hear of them."

Sean was most affected, perhaps, but he showed little of the loss in his behavior except for an unnatural silence. With the strike dragging to its weary conclusion, he had idle time on his hands, time to think and brood. While his father might excuse Taggart, *he* did not. Taggart was the murderer of his brother. Something was gone from his life which could not be replaced and Taggart was responsible. He should kill the man. It was a foolish thought and he knew it. But he found himself less in sympathy with his father and more with those whom his father despised. The Mollies would take care of Taggart. He hoped they would. He hoped he would hear one morning that Taggart was discovered lying in the street, a bullet in him, like Niall. The informer, Matt Silk, was paid off this way but Taggart still lived. There would be a day for him, too.

There were fewer marches now. The miners were ragged and hungry and they were stumbling on the edge of defeat. A few desperate, pointless murders still occurred with shocking regularity. A young miner named Thomas Sanger was killed the first day of September near Raven's Run Colliery in Schuylkill. A friend, William Uren, came to his rescue and was also slain. Five men were suspected but no arrests were made. Two days later, John P. Jones, foreman of the Lehigh and Wilkes-Barre Coal Company, was accosted on the Lansford railway platform by two men who emptied their pistols into him, killing him instantly.

By now the strikers were an army of skeletons, their wills broken, their bodies crippled by starvation, their homes abodes of sorrow and despair. The food was gone and hope went with it. Even Captain Mike neared the last of his savings. Meanwhile, Gowen had not budged an inch and the other owners stood fast by him, refusing to negotiate. The miners met and their feeble organization disintegrated. Some voted for immediate return. The protest diminished and soon there was a mass exodus back to the pits. Although their rebellion had been broken, they could still sing and write ironic poetry.

Well, we've been beaten, beaten all to smash,
And now, sir, we've begun to feel the lash
As wielded by a gigantic corporation,
Which runs the commonwealth and ruins the nation.

And thus the matter stands. We do not dare
To look a boss in the face and whisper "Bah!"
Unless we wish to join that mighty train
Of miners wandering o'er the earth like Cain.
And should you wish to start upon a tramp,
O'er hillock, mountain, valley, plain and swamp,
Or travel as the Pilgrim of John Bunyan,
One talismanic word will do it, "Union."

Those who had been leaders in the strike—men like Roarity and Kerrigan, and John Kehoe of Schuylkill, and Patrick Hester of Centralia, and others—were blacklisted. No jobs were open to them in the coal fields and no jobs anywhere within the influence of the men who owned the mines. Some were forced to flee with their families. Some were later reemployed but became the targets of abuse from every petty superintendent and overseer. Humiliation and ridicule were their daily lot and they were assigned the most dangerous and least profitable working places.

Some, like Roarity and Kerrigan, stayed on to fight. The spark of rebellion remained and the secret societies increased their membership. Every town had a local "bodymaster" or unit leader and, while there was no top coordinating leadership, the individual units exchanged information and performed duties for each other. Meetings were clandestine and the practice of importing killers from neighboring regions crept in. The term "Molly Maguires" became synonymous with death and destruction.

On the first day back at work, some of the miners had gathered near the main shaft, observing the approach of Captain Mike. Taggart stood nearby and they anticipated trouble. Again they were disappointed, for Mike methodically picked up the tags for labeling his cars of coal, shouldered his pick, and entered the cage. The others followed in silence. Taggart never glanced up at Mike but he knew he was there. He could feel it. Although not afraid of Mike, he shuddered involuntarily as the cage disappeared below.

Sean was roaming the streets since no work had yet piled up for the breaker. Sometimes it was like this, even during a busy season. And when there was no coal, there was no work for the breaker boys. And no pay.

Sean's course took him past the hotel, the newspaper office where headlines posted in the window proclaimed the owners' victory, and down to the railroad station. He decided to wait here and watch the early morning train arrive. It pulled in minutes later—a mere hour behind schedule.

First off the train were a couple of businessmen whom Sean classed as dudes, friends of the owners and therefore despicable. They were the enemy. With every day his thinking matched more and more that of his deceased brother. He watched the men go past in their striped suits and clean spats and he glowered fiercely at them. One of them took notice, smiled wryly, and flicked his cigarette in Sean's direction. Both men laughed.

Then some women descended the steps, gaily dressed and returning from a pleasure trip to Philadelphia. There was a boy his own age but scrubbed clean, clad in a silk suit, and carrying a straw hat. The boys exchanged embarrassed glances.

When the train had nearly emptied, Sean's attention was caught by a young redheaded man with a cloth satchel who skipped airily down the train steps. He was simply dressed but had a sparkle about him that defied the cheap clothing. About medium height, he was trim and light on his feet. When he walked, he fairly danced, his blue eyes taking in the town with apparent approval. Sean found something fascinating in the man and he stared at him rudely until the stranger strolled over to him.

"Well, now, have I the look of the criminal about me, lad?" His brogue was thick and lilting, a voice to match the first lively impression.

"No—no, sir. I was only—only watchin' the people off the train."

"Is there no work then for a lad like yourself on a day as lovely as this?"

"None, sir. The breaker ain't operatin' yet, what with the strike just bein' over."

The man nodded. He had a mocking little smile that tugged first at the corners of his mouth before pulling his whole face into a grin.

"But there's work I hope for a strong feller who's after a spot in the mines?"

"I'm sure there'll be."

"Ah, good." The stranger lowered his satchel and extended his hand. "James McKenna is the name but Red will do as well."

Sean smiled and took the proffered hand. "I'm Sean Flannery, Mr. McKenna."

"Call me Red, lad. It's the custom."

Sean laughed. He took an immediate liking to this stranger. "All right, Red."

"Where does a man go when he has a thirst? Would you be knowin' that, Sean?"

Sean paused. "Well, there's Carroll's Saloon but I don't know as I'd recommend it to a stranger."

"And why is that?"

"My pa says it has a bad reputation. There's fights there near every day and twice as many at night."

McKenna's face broke into a grin. "The very place, then. I'm a man who loves a bit of action and it's been a long, stiff ride." He stretched himself to emphasize the point.

Sean scanned the little figure before him, mentally comparing it with the powerful men who ripped coal from beneath the earth. Although it didn't seem a sensible thing to do, he shrugged and offered to show him the way.

They jogged along together up the street, Sean trying to match the light step and holiday air of his companion.

"Sean, another thing. Do you know where there'd be a room for a fellow the likes of meself?"

"The hotel's next to the saloon, Red."

McKenna shook his head. "Now then, I can't abide hotels and would rather sleep in the fields. It's a proper home I'm after, like I've always been used to, Sean. None of these hard beds and sober faces for me. There's the money, too. I've some, to be sure, and can pay me way once I'm located, but not enough for that fancy livin.'"

Sean thought about his own room with the vacant bed where Niall once slept. Suddenly and unaccountably, he wanted this carefree stranger to share it with him. Besides, the money would be welcome after these bad months.

"Maybe I can find somethin' for you. But yonder's Carroll's place. You go on in now and I'll be back. Have a care, like I said."

"I'll be like a mouse before cats. But don't you hurry, for it's been a long dry journey." As Sean dashed off, Red looked up and read the saloon sign with relish, then sauntered inside.

Only one table was occupied. Kerrigan was engaged in a listless poker game with Bully Frazier, a gigantic man with a well-deserved local reputation for violence. Carroll hovered over them, soberly attentive to the play. When McKenna entered, they scarcely looked up.

Not one to tolerate this breach of etiquette, the redhead shrugged, dropped his satchel with a thump, and cleared his throat noisily. Then, in a rollicking tenor voice, he commenced to sing.

> Beauing, belleing, dancing, drinking,
> Breaking windows, cursing, sinking,
> Ever raking, never thinking,
> Live the Rakes of Mallow.

> Spending faster than it comes,
> Beating waiters, bailiffs, duns,
> Bacchus' true begotten sons,
> Live the Rakes of Mallow.

It was a gay, prancing tune and he sang it well, ending in a flourish that was the start of a jig. Soon he had Carroll smiling and clapping the rhythm as he whipped across the barroom floor, thumping his feet to a whistled tune. Kerrigan and Frazier stared, wondering if he were mad, but McKenna continued, kicking his heels in a wild reel.

When he spun to a stop, Carroll applauded vigorously and Red McKenna bowed like the star at an opera. With scarcely a pause for breath, he launched into an encore, mingling English and Gaelic in a tribute to "the cruiskeen lawn," the "little full jug."

> Then fill your glasses high,
> Let's not part with lips a-dry,
> Though the lark now proclaims it's dawn;
> And since we can't remain,
> May we shortly meet again,
> To fill another cruiskeen lawn, lawn, lawn,
> My charming little cruiskeen lawn.
> Gra machree ma cruiskeen,
> Slainte geal mavourneen,
> Gra machree a coolin bawn.
>
> Gra machree ma cruiskeen,
> Slainte geal mavourneen,
> Gra machree a coolin bawn, bawn, bawn,
> Gra machree a coolin bawn.

Another jig followed and another song. For fifteen minutes he provided them an impromptu entertainment featuring "Molly Brannigan," "Johnny, I Hardly Knew Ye," and "The Star of the County Down." Again there was appreciative applause from Carroll and a puzzled response from his two customers.

"Ah, now." Red swung his hand out in a grand gesture. "You're a darlin' audience and I hope I've earned meself a drink."

"You have indeed." Carroll clapped him affectionately on the back. "And my treat. The name's Carroll and I run the place. Them there is Kerrigan and Frazier."

Red bowed and waved. "Red McKenna." He introduced himself.

"I've not heard singin' like that since Ireland. You're a strollin' singer perhaps?"

"Not a bit of it. Sure, I'm a proper miner and I come lookin' for to work."

Kerrigan snorted and McKenna gave him a quick, hurt glance.

Carroll scratched his head. "Minin's rough work. You ever done any?"

"I have indeed. At Tower City, Port Clinton, and elsewhere."

"And before that?" Kerrigan put in.

"You'd like the whole of it, would you?"

Kerrigan nodded.

McKenna sat down on a chair, crossed his legs beneath him, assuming a storyteller's comic pose.

"Born in County Armagh, I was, worked in English factories for a while and devil the bit I liked it. To America I come ten years ago and tried me hand at many things—clerk, teamster, deckhand on a lake steamer, lumberman in Michigan, coachman in Chicago. The lot. Last big job I had was a saloon owner like yourself, Mr. Carroll, and didn't the big Chicago fire in '71 wipe me out, bottles, kegs, and all."

"Then you come here?"

McKenna arched his eyebrows and pursed his lips. Cautiously, he peered around the room.

"You all be friends here, I suppose?"

"Of course."

McKenna sighed. "There was some trouble. The law has been doggin' me footsteps all along. In Buffalo, I killed a man, God rest his soul. Then there was the matter of takin' the two army pensions which the U. S. government frowned upon. And last, there was a quarrel with authorities over the color of me money. A real pity, that last, for I made it meself and it was prettier than the real thing."

Carroll roared in amusement at the rash escapades and even Kerrigan and Frazier had to smile.

"Care to sit in?" Frazier indicated an empty chair.

"I do, indeed, for another of me vices is the cards. Me mother swore I'd never have a lucky day and, by the stool I'm sittin' on, she's been mostly right." He rubbed his hands together and watched Kerrigan shuffle the cards.

When Sean returned, he found his friend defying his mother's grim predictions and in possession of an impressive pile of silver coins. His cheerful smile contrasted noticeably with Kerrigan's frown and the gathering anger of Bully Frazier. Sean remained in the doorway, waiting to catch McKenna's eye. He was uncomfortable in these surroundings and feared his father might discover him. From behind the bar, Carroll winked knowingly and Sean managed a weak grin.

Just then Frazier slammed his cards on the table with his

big, hairy fist. "There ain't been a decent hand dealt me since you sat in, McKenna!"

Red shrugged innocently. "Sure, there's no cause to blame yourself. You've been trying hard enough. What with dealin' off the bottom and all, I mean."

The burly miner leaned across the table toward McKenna, towering above him. "You accusin' me of cheatin'?"

McKenna showed no alarm but merely studied his cards as he replied evenly. "That's the long and short of it. But no harm done since I've a bag of tricks of me own to balance things."

Carroll laughed aloud at the redhead's audacity, which only served to increase Frazier's wrath.

"On your feet, little man. You've a lesson comin' and I'll be your teacher."

Before Frazier could act, Carroll stepped in front of him. "Easy there. This young fellow's a stranger who come peaceful. He don't mean no harm."

"Stand aside." Carroll looked hopelessly at McKenna then stepped back to remove the breakable merchandise from his bar.

"You gettin' up? Or do I learn you where you're sittin'?"

"Heave him out, chair and all," said Kerrigan.

Sean wanted to interfere, to plead for McKenna, but something about the redhead's calm demeanor arrested him.

Red looked at his hand and sighed. "These are right fine cards, gentlemen, and it's a shame not to play them. But first things first." He arose, removed his coat, and tossed it to Sean. Then he confronted Frazier. "I'm ready for that lesson now."

With a great will to oblige, Frazier swung his knotted fist in a vicious arc. But Red was under it and responded with two fast lefts to the bully's nose. Frazier roared, more embarrassed than hurt, and followed with two ferocious swings that ended in the air. McKenna's right cross spread-eagled him over a table. He was up again, punching air. McKenna danced, feinted, teased him with light taps that stung Frazier's ears, eyes, and nose.

Sean hollered in his excitement. "Come on, Red. Again." He sparred nervously, fitting his shadow punches to the action.

A chair crumpled as Frazier again hit the floor. His head rolled against the bar with a thud. One eye was closed, his nose was bleeding, and his face was red from a combination of rage and punishment. He scrambled to his feet unsteadily and waded in again. But the contest which had seemed unbalanced in Frazier's favor, now became a pathetic thrashing of the bully. He found the skilled McKenna impossible to reach whereas he made a constant target for the redhead.

McKenna, smiling all the while, stepped up the pace, flitting out of range, and then darting in close to deliver a tattoo of jabs to the stomach and head. Now he shifted completely to Frazier's midsection, pounding his fists with telling effect. Frazier coughed and grunted, slipped to one knee, and then rose again. His savage swipes became fewer and they carried less steam. As he started to sag, McKenna moved in to finish him. Without losing his pleasant pose, Red threw a battery of punches in combination—rights and lefts, hooks, jabs, uppercuts. They traveled faster than Kerrigan's two good eyes could follow, and much faster than Frazier's one. His arms dropped and Red stood back, shook his head almost sadly, and then rocked him with a terrible blow that upended him. Frazier struggled up on one elbow and then slumped back, unconscious.

Red turned to Carroll in apology. "I'm sorry about the mess." He accepted his coat from the jubilant Sean and then added, "I'd say this calls for a final cup."

Carroll was ecstatic, ignoring the damage in appreciation of the fine brawl he had witnessed. "They're on the house again. You, too, Kerrigan. To the health of a singin', dancin', fightin' redheaded Irishman!"

Kerrigan looked down at Frazier, shrugged and accepted a glass.

McKenna offered a toast. "To the confusion of all mean scuts and cheats."

They drank to that, after which McKenna excused himself and joined Sean at the door.

Carroll called after him. "There'll be a welcome for you here anytime, lad." Then he shuffled over to Kerrigan who was shaking Frazier into consciousness. "There's a boy for you," the proprietor said.

Kerrigan looked at the bat-wing doors, still swinging, and nodded. "I was thinkin' along the same lines meself." He went back to work on Frazier.

Out in the street, Sean was still trembling from the excitement and its unexpected outcome. "Gosh, Red. The toughest miner in the whole town, maybe the whole valley, and you beat him like he was nothin'. He never touched you once."

"Tough he was, but no skill at all, at all. You see, Sean, when you've not the brawn to mix with the big fellows, you must needs have the science."

"Could you teach me?"

Red surveyed him critically, as if appraising his possibilities. "It's likely I could do somethin' for you. But, first, there's the matter of that room."

Sean snapped his fingers. "I near forgot. Ma said you could bunk with me if you've a mind to share our place. It's a big room and two beds."

"What about your pa?"

"He won't mind. No one's used the bed since Niall. He was my brother."

"And he's gone now?"

"He was killed last July." Sean was surprised he could discuss the subject so readily with this stranger. "Taggart shot him. The mine boss."

"I see."

"Then there's only Kitty and me at home besides Ma and Pa. Kitty's my sister and she give her okay, too."

"Then it's settled. It appears the Flannerys have a boarder. Which way?"

Sean gestured down the lane which led into the hills and then swung into stride with his companion. Wasn't he the lucky one to have come upon Red McKenna? And to have him staying at their place, the man who whipped Bully Frazier! Did he fish, Sean wondered. Fish or not, he had a boyish hunch that McKenna's arrival would mean some exciting changes in the Flannery household.

In this premonition, he was entirely correct.

SIX

The Pit

On Thursday, there was work for the breaker boys. Sean sat at his bench, waiting for the rumble of coal to dispel the silence. The heft of his mallet seemed unfamiliar and so did the surroundings after the long layoff.

Brendan was seated across from him. "Begor, I'd like to have seen it, lad. Flattened him like wheat, you say?"

The other boys strained to hear, for the tenth time, the heroic saga of Red McKenna.

Sean brought his story to its glorious end. "Then whoosh, right on the jaw and it was all over and Bully stretched on the floor like a sick mule."

Brendan shook his head admiringly. "Musha, I wish I'd seen it. And where is your dandy today?"

"Pa's takin' him on as his team man. He'll be shovelin' likely. Since Niall died, Pa's had no one. So Red'll come in handy."

Brendan nodded. "Particularly if he can handle that scoop like he done to Bully Frazier."

Their laughter was cut short by a faint churning, like an

army approaching far off. Then it became a roar as the coal burst into the chute, whirling black chunks rattling on the screen and throwing off a cloud of fine dust. For no apparent reason, the boys cheered.

"To work again, lads," called Brendan. Another cycle was beginning. The world turned and the coal hardened. Far away in Ballycotton, it would be dawn and the men would be putting to sea in their bobbing curraghs, with a wind fresh from the bay and the island lighthouse blinking white. Brendan smashed into the black lumps, savagely at first, then mechanically. His gnarled hands, already pale from inactivity, slowly accepted the first coating of grime.

This stream of coal was the legacy of the night shift, now leaving the pit. Mike and Red passed them, a lightly-clad rabble in shorts or breechclothes and caked with sweat and coal dust until only their white, staring eyes protruded. They resembled a safari of African tribesmen, silent—almost sullen—from fatigue.

Red McKenna, like Mike, was dressed in a cotton shirt, open at the throat, wrinkled trousers which disappeared into knee boots and the typical derby-like cap with the torchlight (a little can of kerosene with an exposed wick) near the peak. As they left the pithead, the air met them with a rush, then faded. Prompted by the increasing pressure, McKenna yawned. Then he plunged on in the blackness, listening for the sound of Mike's footsteps in front of him.

Here and there a ledge protruded, jagged and dangerous, or potholes opened beneath their feet. Mike steered Red through the vault, pointing out places he had worked ten and fifteen years before. An occasional stretcher hung on the wooden struts next to a box of bandages. Mules plodded past them, delivering coal to the cage, returning for more. The air became hotter, more humid. An oppressive smell filled the corridors, particularly near the ventilators where the stench was sickening. A few muffled explosions sounded in distant corridors as miners blew coal from the face.

"Just a bit more," said Mike, "then we crawl the rest of the way."

Red nodded. The sweat stood out on his forehead and stained his shirt. His boots were coated with a thick black powder that rose in puffs as they shuffled along and danced in the light of their torches. There was little that could be distinguished—only the timbered walls and ceiling, the murky floor. In the distance, the faint chip of picks mingled with the ventilator hum and the steady chug of the water pumps. The picks became sharper, louder, and now they could hear the scrape of the shovels.

"Watch your head," warned Mike.

They had to double over, their shoulders brushing the tunnel's sides and the light from their kerosene wicks reflecting off the ebony seams. Crouching, groping their way, cramped and uncomfortable, they edged toward one of the chambers off the main feed tunnel. Red gulped air greedily, feeling the atmosphere sitting heavily on him. The odor was fetid and suffocating.

A few more men crept past them. Like the others, they were bathed in sweat and sludge and virtually unrecognizable. One carried a canary in a wire cage, a device used to test for the presence of gas. They moved past, without greeting, as dumbly as the work animals in the main shaft.

As Red and Mike neared their destination, the passage tapered still more. Here there was no shoring but merely a circular tube hewn out of the rock. A rock fall here could be fatal. On their knees now, they inched along, dragging their tools. The rapping of picks and clang of shovels became more distinct. A few caves appeared, hollowed out of the rock walls, and miners were in all of them, pecking away at the coal.

In one depression, a rugged Irishman lay on his back, swinging his pick at the ceiling in a small arc and catching a mouthful of grit for every chunk he dislodged. Seeing a new face, he called to Red, "This is the easy way, lad. But you must work up to it." He laughed and struck again.

In another low cavern, the men were on their haunches, working in teams with an innate rhythm that was fascinating to watch. The picks dived and retreated in unison, rested, then chopped again. Between swings, the shovelers swept in, filling their handcarts. They must be dragged to the main shaft where the mules would handle the remaining transport.

Like knife blades, the keen ridges of the passageway dug into their knees, snatched at their clothing. Red winced but continued on, panting, and the salt sweat burning his eyes. Sidling past them came the last tired remnants of the night crew. Finally they reached a large crypt where half a dozen colliers were assembled and starting in on the "face" of coal. Mike introduced Red around and, since news of his exploit had preceded him, the welcome was genuine.

"Enough gab, then. This here is quota work and you're paid for what you pick, so let's have at it." Suiting action to his words, Mike raised his pick and slammed at the wall. The point dug in. When he wrenched it free, it ripped a stream of coal from the face. Again and again he struck, in explosive bursts, and the coal came shooting out. Red stripped off his shirt as the others had done and called out to Mike. "Lay on there, Mr. Flannery, and I'll be your boy if you dig clear to the river."

Mike laughed and bit into the wall again, showering Red with dust.

"You'll be another color entirely," a miner chided him.

Another joshed, "And no dancin' tonight, I'll wager."

"No fear," Red boasted. "Sure, I could work this face a week straight and then do a month of jigs." He sucked in a mouthful of air and exhaled noisily so they would know he was lying.

That was the end of the talk. Conversation was curtailed in the pit because the air was thin and every breath of value. The only sounds were hollow grunts, the click of tools, and the high-pitched whistle of the ventilator.

Red scooped up the loose coal, tossed it expertly into his cart. His body adjusted to the heat and his lungs to the confining depths. Soon he had established his own working pattern, scraping coal into his shovel and chucking it accurately in one smooth motion. When the cart was full, he dragged it to a large mule car and marked it with the Flannery tag. Then back for more.

Looking around him, Red admired the powerful bodies that shared his labor. All of them showed scars and bruises from rock falls. All displayed rippling muscles, bulging and straining. The black dust billowed around them and their backs oozed perspiration.

At noon there was a brief respite for hard bread and cold sausage. Swigging brackish water from their canteens, they washed down this meager meal and then assaulted the coal face again. Their bodies rocked, steel gleaming from their picks, water glistening on massive shoulders. Punch and recover, scoop and drag. The hours passed, increasing in monotony, constant in punishment. Mike Flannery was a legend in the mines. He never seemed to tire, never swore, and never complained. His quota was always met and his pick always busy. Red knew he had tied in with a man who had no equal and he strove to carry his share.

After nine hours, they were relieved.

"She was about tore out anyway," Mike remarked. "Next crew should cut and blast." He turned to Red, now like a statue carved from coal. "Will you have the stomach for it again tomorrow, do you think?"

There was still some sparkle left in the redhead's eyes. "Why," he said cheerily, "I was real disappointed that you'd knock off so early. I was just getting to enjoy meself." His companions roared and clapped him on the back, making the spray fly.

They crawled out again, slithering through the tunnel to the main shaft. Here they added coal to their last load and led their mule cart up the incline. Another team rolled past hauling a wooden cylinder for sprinkling. The colliers ducked under the water wagon, reveling in its cool jets.

"Had a big dust explosion here right after the war," Mike explained to Red. "Them wagons keep it down pretty well now."

Red nodded. They had reached the pithead and Mike moved his wagon on the scale. It topped two ton—excluding the cart—but the weigher called out, "Ton and a half."

Red stepped forward and inquired pleasantly, "Are you blind, man? The scale says two ton."

Glaring at him, the weigher repeated, "Ton and a half. I can see all right and that load has half a ton of slag in it."

McKenna edged up to him, still smiling. "Mike Flannery don't pick no slag and I don't shovel none. Best you do some refigurin.'"

Just then Taggart walked up and asked, "What's the matter?"

"Flannery's load here is a quarter slag but this bucko claims a full two ton of coal."

"Give it to him."

The weigher protested, "But . . ."

"Do as I say. Credit him with two ton." Taggart walked away, not catching Red's polite little bow behind his back. Resignedly, the clerk noted: "Flannery, two tons."

Moments later they were on the surface and walking home. Other miners were arriving at the cage and they muttered greetings. The sun was low in the west and Pottsville was closing down for the day. A clerk turned the key in the courthouse door and the new storekeeper rolled up his awning. Some women lolled on the steps of their homes, waiting for their men. Children dashed about in enjoyment of the last hours of play.

As Red walked, he could feel his legs tighten and he became conscious of the layer of grime that covered him. But he remained cheerful as he bade good-bye to the men who walked with them.

"Come to Carroll's tonight and have one on Tom Riley," invited a departing miner.

"I may do just that," Red called after him. "Nice fellow," he observed to Mike as they turned into their lane.

"Uh-huh, they're mostly good honest men," Mike agreed. For emphasis, he added, "Mostly."

As the two story frame buildings petered out, shacks began to appear. There were no real streets on the patch since the dwellings were located haphazardly and weeds and brush grew from every crevice. Rocks and coal lay in the pathway and even the trees were scraggly and black.

Mike's home was the finest of a poor lot. In the rear of the rough shanty made of pine slats, stood a welcome tub of water. Sean's head emerged from it, spouting. He shook the drops off like a dog.

"Hi, Pa. Red," he greeted them. "Stew for supper."

"I feel as if I could swallow the cow whole and then eat me way through a field of spuds," Red announced while helping Sean to dry his hair.

Both men plunged head and arms into the tub in turn, sponged off their bodies as well as they could, and prepared for dinner. Before retiring, they would take a dip in the nearby creek for a thorough rinse. In the winter they had only the tub and little privacy.

A simple supper awaited them—the stew, some navy beans, and some biscuits baked in honor of the new boarder.

Mike bent his head forward over his plate.

"Bless us, O Lord, and these Thy gifts, which we are about to receive, from Thy bounty, through Christ, our Lord."

"Amen," they chorused and Red blessed himself with the rest.

Noting this, Mike remarked as he dished up the stew, "We were after figurin' you for a Catholic but one never knows. There's some as has Irish names and devil a good word they have for the Pope or the Church itself."

"Distressing it is, surely," agreed Red, eager to impress the ladies. "My mother was strong for prayers and such and I believe it took on me. I do appreciate a house where such things is honored."

Kitty and Bridget exchanged glances, each secretly beaming at the other.

"And where is your mother now, Mr. McKenna?" Bridget asked. She was on her feet, carefully removing a tray of biscuits from the oven.

"Not far, thank God, in Philadelphia. I write her regular and have hopes of seein' her when the winter is out. My father's dead these five years and I'm all she has."

"A pity, but lucky she is to have you."

"You remind me of her, Mrs. Flannery. I'm a liar if you don't. Same eyes, same smile, same easy way about you."

"Arrah, go 'way with you. The McKennas of Armagh was always known for their blarney."

All joined Red in a good laugh.

"That may be true, Mrs. Flannery, but you have to believe me when I tell you these are the tastiest biscuits I ever popped in me mouth."

"Sure, Kitty baked them. And isn't she the fine hand at cookin'?"

Red shook his head in admiration. "I was about to say—only you'd suspect me honesty—that there must not be another such combination of skill and beauty in all these hills."

Kitty lowered her eyes but smiled. Red McKenna possessed a cheerfulness that disarmed her. Her shyness evaporated. She looked up at him as he winked, not rudely, but with a merriment that was contagious.

McKenna was for extending the mood. "Sean, I tell you what. Would you fancy a walk to town with me this evenin'?"

Mike shot him a stern look of disapproval.

Red lifted his hands in denial. "Never you worry, Mike. I'm not for Carroll's this evenin' but merely out for the exercise and to post a letter to me mother."

"It's all right, then." Sean grinned at his father and dashed off to retrieve his shoes.

Now Red turned to Kitty. "And yourself, Miss Kitty? Would you care to join two wayfarin' bachelors?"

She was surprised at the suddenness of her answer. "Yes, thank you. I'd—love to go."

"Agreed, then." Red clapped his hands. "Now, if you'll hold a few minutes while I write a page, I'll join you. And it's a bath when I return, Mike, so keep the creek warm."

When Red left, Kitty spoke to her mother. "You don't mind do you, Ma? I mean, you havin' to do the dishes and all?"

"Sure not, Kitty child. He seems a likely lad and a stranger needin' directions. You'll be safe enough. How Jimmy Boyle might feel is another thing." Bridget arched her eyebrows coyly.

Kitty stiffened. "Jimmy Boyle doesn't own me and I've seen no ring yet. I expect I can walk with whom I choose."

This outburst brought a chuckle from Mike. "Spoken like a true daughter of your mother."

Her hands on her hips, Bridget flared back. "There's many a man I might have married save yourself, Mike Flannery!"

"And don't I know that, but me natural good looks and promisin' future took you in." Mike gave her hand a squeeze and she relaxed into pleasant embarrassment. "Go on," she said. "You're as bad as the redhead." She sat in his lap and kissed him boldly on the cheek.

Minutes later, Red reappeared and the trio set out for town.

Darkness claimed the hills but a full moon illumined the roadway.

"You must be a scholar to write so much," said Kitty, straining for conversation.

"Not a bit of it. I'm a poor hand with spellin' and I expect either of you could do better."

"Kitty writes good," Sean offered. "She won a prize in school. But my letters is all scrambled."

"You both go to school in town?"

Kitty replied, "For a few years. Pa taught us mostly. And we read whatever we can get."

Red tapped the letter against his palm. "Me mother will rejoice indeed at me good fortune of fallin' in with the Flannerys." He swung an arm around both their shoulders. Kitty discovered she did not disapprove of the gesture but was glad the darkness hid her blush.

"Did you ever hear this tune?" asked Red.

I wish I were on yonder hill,
For there I'd sit and cry my fill,
Till every tear should turn a mill;
Es go deh thu, mavourneen slaun.
Shule, shule, shule agra.

His plaintive tenor rang warm and strange in the night. Kitty fancied she had never heard anything so beautiful—or so sad. Never anything as beautiful and sad.

A sound like distant thunder echoed faintly in the distance.

"They're blastin' the coal for tomorrow," Red said, almost to himself. Then he picked up the thread of the song again.

Soon the three figures were out of sight and only the road remained, washed by the moon like a pale shroud.

Only death can ease my pain;
I long and I long—but I long in vain:
Es go deh thu, mavourneen slaun.

SEVEN

Kitty

On Saturday night in Pottsville, the Welsh miners gathered to smoke their pipes and gossip. Among the English, it was a round of bitter ale at the tavern, a try at the dartboard, and, for an unfortunate few, a piano recital at the civic hall. In Philadelphia, Franklin B. Gowen invited thirty guests for a roast duck dinner. They combined the pleasure of the repast with the business at hand—an efficient method for curbing the continuing violence.

But, in West Patch, the world was reduced to a wee field, rimmed with torches, where the pipers and fiddlers filled the air with a hooting and scraping loud enough to crack a seam of coal. They swept through a chorus of "The Wild Colonial Boy" and followed with "The Star of Donegal." Around the circle of spirited dancers, the old miners and their wives whacked out the beat on their leathery palms. The youngsters whirled and pranced, heads bobbing, curls flying, and legs flicking like frenzied marionettes. Though starless, the evening was cool and invigorating, perfect for the wild, free dancing.

No one cut a more striking figure than Red McKenna. Not a girl but wanted to dance with him and he tried to favor them all, twirling one on the end of his hand, pulling her back again, his feet darting and crossing like angry sparrows. The dancers pulled back, leaving him alone. Red responded with the most ingenious bit of footwork they had ever seen. Beginning with a sudden vault into the air where he clicked his heels twice, he landed on feet already skipping. Pipes shrilled and the fiddlers increased the tempo. Red saluted them without missing a step. There was a nimble, almost feminine, grace about him as he whipped around the ring in a series of dizzy spins. With little regard for tradition, he improvised an assortment of acrobatic feats, weaving them into the jigs and reels. His elbows touched his knees; his legs kicked above his head; a sidestep became a cartwheel. He pumped his legs frantically, thumping the earth and then bounding up again, swinging his arms and hollering, "Hey, hey, hoorah, hey!"

"Dance, avic," the others shouted. Men laughed and older women wept, recalling their own reckless days. They clapped more rapidly and chanted the rhythm in a weird staccato.

"Let 'er rip," cried Sean, who usually glowered silently at the dances in order to avoid the girls.

Faster, faster, Red bucked and stomped, his feet nearly invisible, his legs gone mad. Then, with a final flourish, he spun in the air in a crude pirouette, landed on his knees, and then recoiled into a gay little bow. A terminal shriek on the fiddles and then followed thunderous applause.

For Red McKenna was their darling! Only a month in Pottsville and he had stolen nearly every female heart and won handshakes from every male. Couldn't he sing like a Kilkenny lark? And didn't he have two stories for every one told him? Everything seemed to favor him. When a little girl nearly drowned in the Schuylkill, Red McKenna was there to fish her out. When a rock fall started in Number Three shaft, Red braced the timbers with his back until help arrived. In a fight or a footrace, he was unbeatable. And when he bought drinks for the house, he bragged that the money was counterfeit. "A rare lad," they all agreed.

What's more, there was none to match him with the shovel—or with the pick when he would spell Mike. The Flannery-McKenna combination, always ahead of quota, was reputed the best in the valley. Even Taggart gave him a grudging respect.

Perhaps the sole dissenter was Jimmy Boyle, who saw in Red McKenna only a rival for Kitty. Lacking confidence himself, he imagined his sweetheart as already in love with this "knight of the coalfields."

The legend grew. Even an ordinary visit to a sick friend was liable to erupt into a romantic exploit when Red McKenna was involved. Brendan of Ballycotton repeated this latest venture for an appreciative audience assembled by the row of kegs.

"He'd no more than sat himself down by the bed and was pourin' himself a beer, when in busts Dick Flynn, drunk and ugly, carryin' a forty-four and a knife as long as a pick handle. He has it in for Finnerty, lyin' sick on the cot, and swears he'll kill 'em both. Divil a bit afraid is Red McKenna. Finishes pourin' his beer, he does, and then offers the cup to Dick Flynn as bold as ever you please. The fool reaches for it, of course, and sets down his gun. Movin' like the wind, Red snatches the pistol and fetches Dick a whack alongside the head. Then if he don't lock him in the cellar and call the constable. Sure, it's

Finnerty himself told me and him a sick man watchin' it all."

"A fair evenin's work," said one listener, hoisting his glass.

"McKenna abu!" chorused a couple of others.

Red overheard them and struck a fighting pose, fists clenched, head cocked, and teeth exposed in a fearful grin. They hoorahed again and sent him on his way with another shout, "McKenna abu!"

Kitty was seated alone on a little hillock outside the dancing ring and apart from the boisterous miners. Red slipped up on her.

"You're not dancin'?"

"Just restin' now. Sit you down."

"Sure, me feet is still itchin' and I've a great mind to walk. Will you come with me?"

"I promised Jimmy Boyle the next set."

"Well, I'll not be spoilin' that. But can I be walkin' you home later?"

She peered up at him innocently. "And it only a skip and jump from here?"

"Don't I know that, and me livin' there this past month? But it's a skip and jump I wouldn't trade for an ocean voyage."

Kitty shook her head. "You're a hard man to discourage, Red McKenna, but I'll go along so's you won't lose your way."

"Thank you, ma'am," Red replied with mock gallantry. "I'll be back—for here comes your dancin' partner and I've a feelin' he'd rather see me a few miles from here."

As Jimmy approached, he glimpsed Red's retreating figure. A growing resentment stirred within him.

"It's our dance now, I believe," he said coldly. The bitterness spilled over.

"It is indeed, but you needn't sound like it's a funeral you're attendin."

"I was only wonderin' if you could spare me the time."

Kitty flared. "Jimmy Boyle, there's no call to be rude. Just because you see me talkin' to somebody...."

"Not to somebody. To him. To Red McKenna. Sure, he has you hooked like all o' them others, with his sweet singin' and the gay way about him. You've hardly spoke a word to me all night and it's been the same for weeks. All the while he's courtin' you hisself."

"He is not courtin' me!" She stamped her foot for emphasis.

"It's the same as courtin', then, with him always there and me scarce findin' a chance to talk with you."

"He's a gentleman which is more'n I can say for some."

"You don't know nothin' about him. They say he kilt a man in Buffalo and he's been arrested for shovin' queer money."

"I don't believe it."

Jimmy shrugged. "It's himself has said it."

"That's just his way—to be joshin'. He'd no more kill a man than I would. And you don't believe it either."

Jimmy shifted uneasily. "Maybe not. But I know it ain't been the same between us since he come here. I'm right, ain't I, Kitty? It's not the same." He moved toward her and grasped her shoulders.

"Please, Jimmy."

"You ain't answered me, Kitty."

Kitty sighed inaudibly, her head down and eyes averted from his. "You asked me to dance, Jimmy. Have you forgotten?"

He became conscious of the music, a waltz medley. The last dance. Circling slowly, the torches flickering on their faces, the young men and women of West Patch began their farewells.

Jimmy looked hard at Kitty then. "I guess that's my answer, Kitty. I'll not be botherin' you again." There was no complaint in his tone, only sadness and resignation. Slowly he turned from her and made his way through the dancers.

Kitty whispered softly after him. "Jimmy, I wouldn't hurt you." He was gone. One night—a few words—had dissolved the years they shared. When she looked around, Red McKenna was beside her.

"Didn't I look high and low for you among the dancers and I niver . . ." He checked himself, bewildered. "Kitty, you're cryin'."

"I am not," she lied.

"Well, then, I expect it's the smell from them torches burnin' out. Here, try this." He handed her his pocket handkerchief.

"Thank you." She blew her nose in a most unladylike manner.

"Well, that's better. Tears is for the workin' week. Saturday night is only smiles and songs."

"I'm sorry," she said, sniffing.

"Come along then. We'd best for home. Sean and your folks left half hour ago."

Together they left the field, casting a backward glance at the last dancers. Torches were sputtering and a fiddler yawned impolitely. Saturday night in West Patch was drawing to a close.

For a few yards, the couple walked in silence. Then Red

asked openly, "You quarrel with Jimmy?" Then he added, "You don't have to tell me."

Kitty considered a negative answer but nodded instead. "About me, was it?"

Kitty shrugged. "If it wasn't about you, I suppose it would have been something else."

"But it was meself as caused it."

Kitty made no comment, merely strolled along and then remarked, "Jimmy warned me about you."

"Did he tell you I'm a serpent who steals pretty girls?"

"No. He said you'd killed a man."

Red was silent.

"Did you kill a man? In Buffalo?"

McKenna stopped and turned to face her. "Would it make a difference to you if I did?"

Kitty flushed. "I don't know."

"Well." He started walking again. "There nothin' in it. It's just talk I give the boys."

"I said it was."

Red nodded and then, taking her arm, squired her across the rutted road. He held on to her arm as they approached the Flannery home. A gas light etched one window like a yellow patch on a dark blanket.

"Folks is waitin' up for us," Kitty informed him.

"Let 'em wait a minute more," Red insisted, holding on to her. "Sit a while."

She disengaged herself and sat down. "It's late," she warned.

"I know." Red's mask of humor had lifted, revealing a facet that Kitty suspected, even anticipated, but one which surprised her still. His tone became earnest and quietly appealing.

"Kitty," he continued, "I'll not say I've no words for what I want to say because that would be a capital lie. I've the words all right but none of them makes any sense at all. They keep coming out soundin' like moonlight, and music, and lots of Irish blather. I'll do the straight of it. Ever since I seen you that first night I been dreamin' impossible things, like you bein' the girl for me and us married up and maybe leavin' here for good and all. 'Course I ain't said nothin' on account of Jimmy Boyle but a man keeps his gob shut too long and the vein is played out." He paused and Kitty waited. "I'm the lad with the pretty phrases," he said sheepishly, "but they're somehow choked inside of me. But the meanin' is plain enough. It's . . . that I'm in love with you, Kitty Flannery."

Kitty trembled but couldn't trust herself to match his serious mood.

"You've probably sold the same cabbage to the other girls," she teased. "And maybe it's not your mother you write every week but some colleen in Philadelphia."

"I swear there's no one there. I've not opened me heart to another." He seemed hurt by the light accusation. And Kitty yielded her buoyant pretense.

"Oh, Red," she protested. "Sure, I'm all confused. I don't know me own mind."

"But you do care enough for me not to laugh at me story?"

"You've guessed that already," she said. "But I know little enough about you—where you come from, what you did, where you'll be goin'?"

"There's not so much to tell."

"I'd like to hear it all the same."

"Aye. One day I'll be givin' you the whole story. And I'll not ask your hand until you've heard it. Fair enough?"

"Fair enough." Smiling, she extended her hand to shake, as men would seal a bargain. But Red pulled her to him and kissed her impulsively.

Releasing her, he apologized. "I suppose I shouldn't have done that."

Kitty smiled again. "Good night," she said, entering the house before him.

No sound now came from the little makeshift village. The last lamps died. But Red McKenna sat on the porch, grinning, and he began to whistle. Remembering the late hour, he clapped a hand to his mouth boyishly. As he continued to sit, the serious mood returned. Absently, he picked up a splinter from the porch and toyed with it. His brow furrowed in meditation. Then, weary with thought, he snapped the splinter and tossed it aside. Rising, he went indoors and to the fitful sleep that awaited.

EIGHT

McKenna Meets the Mollies

*R*ain awakened Pottsville on Sunday—a cold, driving rain that tore the first leaves from the trees. October was like this sometimes, flirting with winter like an impatient child.

"Dreary day," Mike Flannery remarked from his doorway. He wore an old army raincoat and Sean, in a canvas slicker, stood beside him. "Come on, or we'll be late for church."

The four Flannerys and Red McKenna stepped into the street, skirting the puddles and feeling the rain chill against their ankles. Kitty, in a gay mood, squealed and shivered. Red took her arm openly and her parents noted this symbol of some change in their relationship. Still, they accepted it naturally. It wasn't to be Jimmy Boyle then. Ah, well, Kitty was a big girl and knew her own mind. And there's not a thing wrong with James "Red" McKenna. They struggled on, skidding sometimes, caking their shoes in mud.

"Watch, Red," cried Sean. "I'm dynamitin' the breaker." He sailed a huge rock at a distant chuckhole and watched as the geyser of water responded.

In tones of reprimand, his father cautioned, "None of that

talk, now. It's Sunday and there's enough rough stuff in the week."

There had been, indeed. A tool shed was blown up in Shamokin, killing the watchman and his young son. Almost within the shadow of Philadelphia, a coal train was derailed and burned. And two prominent members of the Ancient Order of Hibernians were waylaid and hanged on Summit Hill by a band of vigilantes.

Tension mounted in the Mammoth Vein country. It was something you could sense rather than define, like a storm coming or a death in the family. But it was there all right. Activity increased among the Coal and Iron Police and plain-clothes detectives from Scranton and Philadelphia began to appear in the mine towns, asking questions. Even crimes that had occurred years before were quietly and efficiently investigated. Something was in the wind and, this time of year, the wind always blew cold and menacing.

If Red McKenna and Kitty Flannery noticed it, they gave no outward indication. Side by side, they knelt in church, listening to the rain rattling the shingled roof and squeezing through the cracks. No sermon was possible but Father McDermott did read to the congregation a letter from the bishop in Philadelphia.

"I'll not give you the whole text," he explained, "but the simple meaning is one we've talked on often. And that is that anyone who joins with a secret society and becomes involved in the commission of crimes is liable to excommunication. This is a terrible sentence for a Catholic and I trust its message is not lost on you."

After Mass, the miners and their families gathered in little knots under the churchyard trees. Some were waiting out the rain while others were merely glad of the excuse to socialize. They spoke of the bishop's ban and about the recent deaths. It was bitter, desperate conversation for the most part, with water streaming down the stern faces. No one noticed when big Hugh McGehan edged up to Red McKenna and slipped a note into his hand. Even Kitty, standing beside him, missed the action.

"We'll catch our death standin' here," she said.

Red nodded and tucked the note into his pocket. "Let's go, then. Come along, Sean."

They ventured into the streets again, followed by Mike and Bridget. Arm-in-arm strolled Kitty and Red, smiling like schoolchildren as their shoes made sucking sounds in the quagmire. When they reached the Flannery home, their first move was into dry clothes. Once alone with Sean, Red turned his back furtively and scanned the note.

"Carroll's. Tonight at 9:00," was all it said.

McKenna crumpled the paper, held it in his hand for a moment, reflectively, and then tossed it into the coal grate. He continued dressing.

While slipping on a pair of work levis, Sean inquired, "Red, how about that boxin' lesson today?"

Red scratched his head. "Mighty wet for a session, I'd call it."

"Couldn't we spar some indoors?"

"Exceptin' your Pa wouldn't like it. He'd have the hide off me. I take him for a peaceable man with no likin' for fisticuffs,"

Sean nodded. "You're right, I suppose. Funny, Brendan says once my Pa was the most feared man in the mines."

Red was lacing his boots. "He could handle most men still from the looks of him. War changes lots of things. So does a family. But, as me old grandfather used to say, 'The biggest bite's in the quiet dog.'"

Sean laughed. "Maybe tomorrow."

"Right." Red was still thinking of the cryptic message and he smiled.

The day passed slowly. Vagrant winds sloshed rain across the window panes in intermittent gusts. They could hear the creek gurgling behind the house, running full and fast. Limbs creaked and snapped. When Red announced he'd be off for town, the others were understandably surprised.

"Sure, there must be ducks on your family tree," said Bridget. "It's a poor night for the walkin' man."

"Well," joked Red, "it'll save me a bath. And I did promise O'Grady a game of the cards. Hates to go back on me word."

Mike nodded. "We'll leave the door open so. And take me coat here to keep the wind off your back."

"Thanks. I'll not be long."

The mile to Pottsville was one long stretch of mud and a slanting wall of water plunged into it. Red was drenched when he arrived at Carroll's. Behind him, in the hills, he could hear the rumble of approaching thunder. Lightning flickered on the dim horizon. He stepped inside and shed his wet coat.

Only one table was occupied and that by Roarity, Kerrigan, Hugh McGehan, and Jack Kehoe, county delegate of the Hibernians and a local political boss. At their signal, Red joined them. Sitting down and accepting the glass offered him, he remarked, "It was a thin bit of news that Hugh here delivered me."

"But it brought you out on a stormy night," said Jake Roarity.

"Aye," admitted Red, fingering his glass, "I was that curious."

Roarity leaned forward. "No need for keepin' you that way. We've watched you these weeks past and think a lad of your spirit should be one of us. We're askin' you in."

Red extended his hands, palms up in interrogation. "By us, you mean . . . ?"

"Those here that you know, plus fifty more in Pottsville and hundreds and hundreds in the valley."

Red nodded thoughtfully, then smiled. "It's a big honor you do me, surely."

"Then you accept?" asked Kehoe.

"Hold a minute." Red held up a restraining hand. "I've heard nothin' yet but an invite, and I play in no games 'til I've had a look at the cards."

The others glanced at Kehoe, electing him their spokesman. He was a thin man, pleasant, with a full head of dark hair and clouded eyes rimmed with deep circles. He looked like a man recovering from a long illness.

"Unless you be a member," he explained, "there'll be no details on the organization. But we picked tonight because there's to be an initiation here—the back room—within the hour. Just one man. We'd like to make it a pair."

Red sat back, rolling his glass between his palms, indicating he'd like to hear more.

Kehoe studied him a moment, drawing a bony finger across his upper lip, slowly. Then he continued. "As to what we do—you know already. If you don't know, you've heard. We're banded together because the wrongs are too big to right alone; and we're closemouthed because it's worth your job or your life to speak out. There's lots of deeds we do, all pressin' the owners to bring them to decent treatment of the likes of us. Sometimes it's plain political, like at votin' time. Sometimes the game is rougher. We see this as war, McKenna. Us agin' them and no surrender. If you're the lad we think you are, with a taste for action and a stomach for trouble, you'll throw in with us. Sure, we're the only chance the miners got at all."

Red returned his stare, his face a mask.

"Let me add a last thing," Kehoe said. "You've heard many things about the organization—tales of blood and fire and all that. There be some truth to the stories but we're no murderers by choice. Most is like meself, married men, and only in it for the good that can be done. There's distasteful jobs fall to men sometimes and there's got to be men to do them. Me hands may not be clean, but me heart is, I tell you that."

McKenna rocked forward. "Suppose I agree, will this be kept quiet?"

"As the grave. You have our word. But what is it that's botherin' you? The priest? Or is it Captain Mike?"

"It's true that Father McDermott warned us. . . ."

"He's only one," interrupted Roarity. "There's others come out strong for us."

"I can't see as any priest ever hurt ye," countered Red, "but he's not me main worry. It's no secret I'm courtin' Kitty Flannery and, should the Captain find out, he'd have no part of me. I'll not risk that."

"Him that talks is a dead man," promised Kerrigan, speaking for the first time. "You're with us then?"

"God help me, yes. I've seen the same starvin' looks, the same dead bodies by the road. And, by nature, I'm no patient gentleman. So here's to true comrades and a long life to us all." He raised his glass.

"I'll drink to that," said Kehoe and the other followed suit.

Scarcely had they touched the glasses to their lips when the door swung open admitting Jimmy Boyle in a shaft of rain. Red stared at him a moment, then at his companions, before downing his drink.

"It's Jimmy Boyle who's to be the other one," Kehoe explained casually. Through his bleary eyes, he watched for McKenna's reaction.

But Red merely nodded. Thunder rolled through the valley now, like a wagon in the street, and lightning cracked in the dripping forests. Carroll strolled over to secure the door, took a quick look outside, and then ducked back, wiping his face with his apron. Jimmy Boyle stood by the bar, not drinking, and not looking at the others. At Carroll's signal, Kehoe led the men to a back room. It was in total darkness so they fumbled for chairs.

"Over here, McKenna and Boyle," Kehoe directed. They slipped into chairs in front of a smooth pine table. Kehoe faced them, standing, his hands clasped behind his back.

"It's time you hear the laws and the secrets of the organization. In a minute you'll swear to them all and you'll be bound by them. So keep a good ear open. From the first words I says to you, there's to be no talk of it or the others here are sworn to kill you."

A flash of lightning exposed his profile against the room's single window. Wet gusts slapped against the pane.

"Carroll—himself that's tendin' bar—is your 'body master.' His orders is law and you'll get 'em mostly from Roarity here, who'll be contact man. Stay clear of Carroll himself. Comes a time when some other division wants a favor in their town, do as you're bid, no questions, and no cryin' afterward. They'll return the gesture, no fear. Our aim is to kill no one unless orders call for it or you has to do so to save your neck. But carry arms any time you're out 'cause you're a marked man when you step out of here."

He paused, looked out a minute at the storm, and went on.

"When you shall see a man on the street and want to know if he's friend or not, why, you takes the little finger of your right hand and puts it next the outside of your right eye. If he's a fellow member, he'll take your right lapel in reply, usin' the thumb and little finger on his right band."

"And in the dark?" asked Red.

"When you're not able to see a man, you say to him, 'The Emperor of France and Don Carlos of Spain,' and he'll come back with, 'May unite together and the people's rights maintain.'"

Red stirred uneasily and tried to see Jimmy Boyle in the dark. Ironic that they should be enlisting at the same time. Again lightning illuminated the room, exposing Jimmy's boyish face, now set and determined.

"Suppose you're enterin' another division of this order," continued Kehoe. "The password is, 'Will tenant right in Ireland flourish?' and the answer should be, 'If the people unite and the landlords subdue.' On dark nights, such as this here, just say, natural-like, 'The nights are very dark' and a friend will reply, 'I hope they will soon mend.' Then there's one more— the quarrelin' word. If you've started into a fight and wonder if maybe the other man's a member, tell him, 'Your temper is high.' If he's O.K., he'll come back with, 'I have good reason.' Do you have them now?"

The two recruits nodded affirmatively in the dark, their silence carrying assent.

"Good," said Kehoe. "Then we'll be about swearin' you in.

Your orders will come later and we've a bit of business to conduct before we leave."

Kehoe then outlined the laws and purposes of the society, laying stress on the qualities of "friendship, unity, and true Christian charity" and the exclusion of any member for any "atrocious offense."

"Stand now," he ordered, "and repeat this pledge after me. You first, McKenna. Then yourself, Jimmy Boyle."

Slowly, Red echoed the words of Jack Kehoe, pronouncing them carefully above the roar of the storm.

"I, James McKenna, having heard the objects of the order fully explained, do solemnly swear that I will, with the help of God, keep inviolably secret all the acts and things done by this order, and obey the constitution and bylaws in every respect. Should I hear a member illy spoken of, I will espouse his cause, and convey the information to him as soon as possible for me to do so. I will obey my superior officers in everything lawful and not otherwise. All this I do solemnly swear."

"Now you, Boyle."

In a clear but strained voice, Jimmy Boyle gave back the pledge as it was given to him. "All this I do solemnly swear," he concluded.

Another bolt crashed nearby, splitting a tree and causing them to start up.

"Pull the shade there," commanded Kehoe, "and have Carroll bring up the lamp. We'll go over our business presently."

The tavern owner entered with the lamp and set it upon the table, throwing a soft yellow glow on the conspirators. He shook hands with McKenna and Boyle, congratulating them.

Kehoe, meanwhile, unrolled a crude map onto the flat surface.

His long, tapering finger found a pencil mark. "This is Catawissa–about 30 or so miles north of here. Any of you know it?"

"I been there," volunteered McKenna.

"You know the railroad bridge?"

"Uh-huh. I seen it some time ago but I recall it has a triple span across the river–the Susquehanna River."

"That's it," returned Kehoe, pleased. "It belongs to the Pennsylvania railroad–Gowen's outfit–and it would cost him a fat lot were something to happen to it."

"Like getting itself blowed up?" Kerrigan put in.

Kehoe smiled. "Exactly. It'll take the lot of you to pull it off. Jake will be in charge with McGehan and Kerrigan and both of you." His finger jabbed at McKenna and Boyle. "You must get a look at it first. Since you been there, McKenna, I suggest you give it a scout next weekend."

"When do you figure to blow it?" asked Kerrigan.

"Soon after that as we can. Maybe a week Tuesday. Depends on how it looks."

"Curiosity only," said Red, "but why do we go so far away–thirty miles–to blow a bridge?"

"It's like I mentioned, a favor for another division."

"Does seem a long way, agreed Carroll. "A long way to carry explosives and a long way to sneak back."

Kehoe faced them sternly and concluded the argument. "It's the Miners' Union asked for it. Or, leastwise, one of their officers. It's owed to them."

Carroll shrugged and said, "Let's look at the map."

Kehoe pointed out Catawissa, located on the rolling plain

drained by the Susquehanna. To the south lay the Blue Mountains and the coalfields.

"There's a crossroads here, one road leadin' south to Pottsville, the other east and southwest between Scranton and Harrisburg. The bridge is this side of town." He traced the route with his forefinger.

"Couple dozen sticks on the center span should take her down," Kerrigan suggested.

"That's your department, Powder Keg," said Kehoe. "But, first, Red checks the place. Go by what he finds out."

When all questions had been answered, Carroll spoke. "That'll be all for now. We meet here a week from Monday night for Red's report." He blew out the lamp, returning the room to darkness. "One more thing. I might as well be straight out and say what's on my mind. Maybe there be differences among some here, but in organization business you act together."

Jimmy Boyle spoke up for the first time. "You thinkin' of anyone in particular?"

"I am," Carroll returned evenly. "McKenna and yourself."

They stood quietly in the dark, the rain pounding the roof above them and the thunder moving south to shake Tremont and Pine Grove and Tower City.

"I joined to fight Gowen," said Jimmy, "not for a private quarrel."

"Then shake his hand," Carroll ordered.

Red McKenna waited, his hand extended in the gloom. The others waited, too, breathing huskily in the cramped space.

Jimmy Boyle spoke again. "I said I'd not fight McKenna, but neither will I shake his hand. He means nothin' to me, no more'n a dog. I'll work with him agin' the mine owners but I'll not shake his hand."

"It's all one with me," McKenna cut in, breaking the tension. "I'll do me job and I expect all others will do theirs." He opened the door and stepped into Carroll's empty taproom. The others followed, leaving the tavern singly and heading home their separate ways. Red plodded toward West Patch, his borrowed raincoat whipping about his damp ankles and the wind driving slivers of rain against his face. Fading thunder growled like a retreating animal.

"And if she finds out," Red said to himself. "If she does, will it be over with us?"

He slogged along, head down, lost in thought.

NINE

The Bridge at Catawissa

A week later, Red McKenna rented a carriage and he and Sean Flannery went fishing.

"They tell me the trout are large as bread loaves near Catawissa," Red exclaimed as they drove away after Mass. "I'll see a cousin there on business and then we'll have the rest of the day to ourselves." The road cut through the mountain, bright with fall colors. The air was crisp and the sun danced on the leaves. Beyond the ridge of hills stretched the tilled fields, now dull and gray after giving up their treasure. A small stream kept pace with them for a time, running beside the road, hurtling little rocks, and washing the base of scrub oaks that clung to the bank. Once, when they looked up, they saw flights of ducks heading south, like arrowheads etched in the sky. By noon, they had reached Catawissa and found a place just below the bridge to set their lines. As Sean tended the poles, Red excused himself and disappeared into town. An hour later he returned.

"Catch anything?"

"Not a nibble."

"Not our lucky day, I guess. My cousin was out, too. Looked all over for him but . . ." He left the sentence unfinished.

"What line of work is he in, Red? Your cousin?" Sean kept one eye on the bobbing corks.

"My cousin? Oh, he's—he's a watchmaker. Makes watches, fixes clocks and such."

"Must be a smart man."

"Oh, he is. He is, indeed."

Sean toyed with one of the poles thoughtfully. "How'd you like that work, Red?"

"Fixin' watches?"

"Anythin' like that. Livin' in a town outside the mines. Comin' home from work clean."

"I've lived like that, Sean boy." Red pulled a long stalk of grass and sat down, sucking on the smooth stem. "I had jobs in cities. Lots of cities. And in big ones, like Chicago."

"And didn't you like it?"

Red shrugged. "I suppose. One job is the same as another."

"Not the mines though. I don't expect anythin' else is like the mines. Pa says it's the dirtiest work on God's earth. And the hardest, for the smallest pay. Niall used to say it was all to make a few men rich while we was slaves like."

"And you'd be partial to Niall's views."

Sean nodded. "He was right, too. Pa couldn't see it but I seen it all along. Niall was right about everything."

"Bein' right got him killed."

"Maybe. But he done a man's job."

Red decided to switch the subject. "Give a little jerk on that line. I thought I seen somethin'."

A quarter of an hour passed with Sean concentrating on the elusive fish and Red sitting, quietly, and stealing a look at the boy periodically. He broke the silence. "Sean, did you ever see a man killed?"

Sean looked up, surprised. "I saw my brother after Taggart shot him."

"Wasn't pretty, was it?"

"No, sir."

"Them that gets kilt on both sides looks like that, Sean. And someone always has to do the shootin', or the stabbin', or the burnin.' You think you could do it?"

Sean hesitated, looked across the river into Catawissa. "I don't know, Red. I think I could."

Arising, Red came over to him and threw an arm around his shoulder. "I don't think you could—now or ever. And it's a good thing, like as not. Come on, the fish aren't bitin' today. Let's drive on back and try again another day."

They tossed the poles into the carriage and Red snapped an order to the black mare. Soon they were churning down the road in a whirl of dust and Red was singing at the top of his tenor voice.

A plenteous place is Ireland for hospitable cheer,
     Uileacan dubh O!
Where the wholesome fruit is bursting from the barley
          ear;
     Uileacan dubh O!
There is honey in the trees where the misty vales
          expand,
And her forest oaths, in summer, are by falling waters
          fann'd,

There is dew at high noontide there, and springs i' the
        yellow sand,
On the fair hills of holy Ireland.

Their carriage swept through sprawling farmland. Naked
stalks of corn poked out of the earth and the ripple of fresh
furrows climbed small rises and then burst into the flat like
rays from the sun. Occasionally they passed a farmer driving
his team and they waved to him. Or they glimpsed husky
German boys sitting before their cottages mending harness
or wives churning butter. The harvest was over and the land
was being readied for the next season. In the mines there was
only the season of darkness—sometimes chill, often hot. But
on the land the months had meaning. There was a time for
planting and a time for reaping. You watched the sky for rain
and you watched the infant seeds sprout green and yellow.
On steamy August nights you could hear the corn popping
among the cricket sounds. Best of all would be the days when
you rode behind the span of horses, their heads down, exud-
ing power. You felt their power in the reins and saw the blade
beneath you rip into the earth like a steamer in clear water.
Hard work, yes! But on the earth, not under it. You saw clouds,
smelled rain, sifted rich loam through your fingers. You cre-
ated things and you tasted the crisp results of your labor.

These were Red's thoughts as they jogged along. "You talk
about livin' in a town." He pointed toward the fields. "Now
right there is the life. A sure enough farm with a wee cottage
and nothin' your hand touches but don't belong to you."

"Well, then, why don't you try it, Red?"

McKenna shrugged. "No funds to buy it. No skill to run it.
No courage to set about it in the first place."

"Jimmy Boyle used to talk about goin' west and farmin' the free land in Nebraska or the Dakotas or maybe further west."

The thought of Jimmy Boyle stopped him a second, but Red replied. "If you've a mind to starve and thirst and fight Injuns all day, I suppose it might do. You read the papers and every day it's one a them tribes scalpin' settlers or massacrin' soldiers. I like me hair the way it is—red and fastened to me skull."

"I guess it would be hard, but nothin' comes easy."

Red was pensive momentarily. "No," he agreed at last. "Nothin' comes easy." This closed the conversation. Ahead of them lay the autumn hills and then home.

On Monday evening Red kept his appointment at Carroll's saloon. All the others were there, save Kehoe, who was not in this division. Red's report was brief, factual, and concluded with the advice that an attack on the bridge would be unwise.

"Everywhere I looked in town," he said, "there was police. It's almost as if they was waitin' for trouble."

"Was the bridge itself watched, do you think?" asked Roarity.

Red nodded. "The whole time I was there, pretendin' to be fishin', I could see a couple of blacklegs pacin' on the other shore, keepin' an eye on me."

"How about at night?" Kerrigan asked. "Could you slip in then and do the job?"

"Maybe," said Red, "if you know the bridge. Even then it would be risky. Anyway, I just don't think we can blow that bridge anytime and get away with it." He said this slowly and emphatically.

"Why not?" Carroll put in. "It's just a bridge, like all the others."

Red pushed back his chair, propping his knees against the table. Carroll had closed the bar early and they were alone. Red swept all the quizzical faces with a single glance before speaking.

"It's like I said. They seemed to be expectin' somethin'. I smell a trap for us all. And I'm thinkin' further that it was planned this way by the mine union so's we'd get caught."

"For a young feller," said Carroll sarcastically, "you done a lot of thinkin'."

Roarity came to Red's support. "It may be he's right. It's little enough help the union was this year past. And with us gettin' stronger, it could be they'd welcome our trouble."

"You're talkin' nonsense," Carroll protested. But his eyes betrayed his own doubts.

"Am I, now?" persisted Jake Roarity. "Who criticizes the order in the papers? And who puts in words against us with the governor there in Harrisburg? And who was it told us to go back to the pits when we was first out? The mine union is who. And with us starvin' on the strike, not one rotten cent did they send us. They'll send no flowers if we was strung up at Catawissa."

"You ain't bein' quite fair, Jake," Carroll argued, but his tone was uncertain.

"Maybe it ain't the whole story but I seen enough to think Red here is as right as four aces in a poker game."

"You for forgettin' the whole scheme?" asked Carroll.

Roarity looked around. "I'd go with the vote, of course, but puttin' in my two cents now, I'd say, yes, let's chuck it."

The others nodded and Carroll acquiesced. "All right," he

said. "I'll tell Kehoe. And I hope you're right, Red McKenna."

"I give you only me report and me own thinkin'," Red reminded him. "Sure, I've not been around long enough to know the mine unions like Roarity here."

The enterprise collapsed. It was a bad beginning to their work and it had some sequels which were equally ineffective. One was a murder attempt on William Thomas of Mahanoy City. Thomas was one of the many men bitter about the acquittal of Dan Dougherty for the shooting of George Major during the fire company riot. For months he had bullied Dougherty who could not flee nor could he go to the police. He turned instead to the Molly Maguires.

McKenna, along with John Gibbons, Michael Doyle, and Thomas Hurley, trekked to Mahanoy City and staked out their victim. But militia were in town to guard against a threatened strike and Red thought the time inopportune.

"So you weren't able to kill a single man—the four of ye?" Kehoe mocked them when they returned.

"God's truth," Hurley blurted. "Them blacklegs was fair swarmin' in the town. We hadn't no chance at all."

Kehoe reprimanded him with a searing glance. "If you've no stomach for this work . . ."

The quartet growled uncomfortably. "Give us another chance," said Gibbons. "We'll wrap him in his shroud."

"Oh, you'll have your chance all right. It's a debt owed Dougherty. You settle this, McKenna. Pick your time and place but I want Bill Thomas out of the way." He got up and left them, the doors fluttering angrily behind him.

No one moved for a time. Their heads were lowered, some in anger, some in shame. But Red McKenna snapped them out of their lethargy.

"He puts me in mind of a landlord in Kerry who had two contrary tenants, one a silly boy and the other an old widow. One day. . ." And he spun out the yarn, gesticulating, acting the parts, bringing tears of laughter from his audience. When he'd finished he capped the story with a word of advice. "The moral bein', if you don't succeed at first, why then, you must try again."

"When?" asked Hurley. He had an empty pistol tucked in his belt and was strumming the hammer nervously.

Red thought for a moment. "Today, a week."

"At night, is it?"

"No," replied Red, making a sudden decision. "We'll go over there in the mornin'. Not show at work or come in late. There'll be less danger then."

"Yours is the word," agreed Hurley. "Monday, then." The others nodded and then left McKenna alone with James Carroll. Red rubbed his finger along the edge of his glass. He was thinking of the bridge and the triple span and the shallow water with few fish.

"How you gettin' on at Flannery's?" Carroll asked. He was leaning over him, swabbing the table with a checkered rag.

"Well enough."

"Kitty's a darlin' girl. And her father—Captain Mike—a good man. A very good man. We tried to join him up but he'd have none of it. We figured when Niall was shot. . ."

Reading his thoughts, Red commented, "Sure, he was more set against you than ever. It's not the owners he blames for the boy's death but yourselves."

Carroll nodded thoughtfully. "Do you think you might bring him in, Red? He's a likin' for you. All can see that. It would be a very big thing. There's a lot thinks like him and we could maybe win them, too."

"No, that's not a job for meself. Besides, we'd be after wastin' our breath like snow on a river. He's set agin it, I tell you, and won't change."

Carroll tossed the rag behind his bar and scowled. "Aye, I suppose you're right but it pains me sorely. There's them as keeps their hands clean and souls white while others does their work. And who profits? The quiet ones in the end. They're committed to nothin' and don't raise a finger to help themselves or others."

Red cocked his head in disagreement. "Captain Mike was in the war. He took sides then and fought bravely. He has a family now, man. Responsibilities."

Carroll swore. "I have a family, too." Then, softer, he added, "Aye, Red McKenna, I have a family too, and it's them I'm thinkin' of." This ended the discourse, with Carroll retiring behind his bar to cap the spigots. Red downed his drink, tossed a coin on the bar, and strolled out.

A week later, McKenna lay in bed, complaining of a headache and fever. Sean and Mike left at dawn for the mines, carrying their tools and their salt pork lunch.

"A speedy recovery," Mike said to the patient.

"Just a chill, I expect," Red answered cheerfully. "I'll be well tomorrow. But easy on the pick, Mike, for I'll be a weak man and not able to face up to that big pile of coal."

After they left, Kitty brought him some coffee, kissed him lightly on the forehead, and departed. Red settled back to await Hurley's knock. There had better be Hurley only. He told them to send but one man for him.

"Rap! Rap!" Softly and politely the knock came. Bridget

was scrubbing clothes in the backyard, so Kitty opened the door. Hurley was there, cap in hand and grinning sheepishly.

"Is Red McKenna about, ma'am? I'd like words with him."

"He's in bed with a sickness, and not able for work. You're a friend of his, then?"

"I am." Hurley tried to sound as solicitous as possible. "And it's sorry I am to hear of him sick. Could I be seein' him?"

She hesitated.

"For a moment only."

"Well, I suppose it's all right. Come in." Hurley followed her inside and through the burlap curtain. She left the men alone.

"Hullo, Tom."

"Hullo, yourself. It's after six and time to be off." Hurley kept his voice low. "Gibbons and Doyle is waitin' by the fork and I brought along a fellow named Morris. He's a crack shot."

Red twisted in his bed and frowned slightly. "Tom, I can't make it this day. Fever's got me weak as a split shovel."

Concerned now, and a little frightened, Hurley moved closer. "Sure, I thought it was only a dodge to get out of work. Are you really sick, then?"

"I've a fierce headache and my stomach is grinding queer-like."

Hurley pawed his chin nervously, trying to think. Without McKenna, it might be more dangerous. Still, they had failed once and couldn't wait forever.

"Will you be about tomorrow, do you think?"

Red lifted his hands in a gesture of uncertainty. "I dunno."

Still Hurley hesitated. "We got the guns and all. The others will be wonderin'."

"Go on, then. There's Morris with you so you won't need

me. Watch for the police, though, and take no long chances."

"Well . . . okay, then. We'll tackle it. But I do wish you was along." He moved toward the curtain.

"Luck," McKenna called after him. Hurley turned and waved but his mouth was set and unsmiling. When he had disappeared, Kitty re-entered the room.

"I've never seen him before. Is he a friend from Carroll's place?"

Red nodded. He was still brooding over the visit. His hands were locked behind his head and he had sunk deep into his pillow. When Kitty spoke again, he scarcely heard her.

"I was that worried, Red. Truly, I was. There's been some talk you was mixed up with the Mollies. I know it's silly but I hear Pa sayin' it to Ma."

Red switched his gaze to her but said nothing.

"It ain't so, is it, Red?"

McKenna forced himself to smile. Sitting up, he touched her hand with his. "Sure, and if it was, wouldn't you be the first to know? Wouldn't I be tellin' you right now?"

She regarded him seriously, her eyes kind and patient. "I hope you would. It's that I know so little about you—your family, your life before here, even your friends."

Red took her by the shoulders and grinned broadly. "You'll know it all when you're Mrs. McKenna—every last detail of me sinful life."

Kitty dropped her eyes to her hands, focusing on the white knuckles. "When will that be, Red?"

He seemed surprised, as if the thought were a new one. "When you're Mrs. McKenna, you mean?"

She nodded.

He forced her to look up at him. There was no devilish

grin now, only a soft solemnity about him. "Would April suit you, Kitty darlin'?"

Again she nodded, but with a difference this time. Tears formed in her eyes. He pulled her close to him. "April it is, then. I'll have enough saved for a honeymoon in Philadelphia. Does that strike your fancy, Miss Kitty Flannery? Or do them tears say you regret ever meetin' me?"

She kissed him quietly, thanking him with her lips for all that he meant to her.

"There now, you'll catch whatever I've got. Be off and say nothin' yet. Christmas will be time enough to tell them all." She backed out the door and he could hear her softly singing as she went about her chores. Moments later there was another knock and Hurley was ushered back into the room.

Red was startled. "I thought you had gone along with your friends."

"Well." Hurley turned first to Kitty and then to Red with an expression of infinite compassion. "I thought of you lyin' here with all day before you and knowin' how you like the cards, I thought I might spend a few hours with yourself."

"That's very kind of you," Kitty said with sincerity. "I'll put on some tea." She made her exit again.

"Is this your idea, Hurley?" Red asked as his companion began shuffling a deck of stained cards. "It's little you care for me health but you're here to watch me like a criminal."

Hurley was embarrassed by the accusation. "I'll not lie to you, Red. But it's an order rule. You'd have to do the same to me, was our places exchanged. It's just a rule."

"Then deal yourself a lone hand. I'm not after playin' with anyone who mistrusts a comrade." Red turned away.

"Aw, Red." Hurley protested but he was afraid to leave. He

dealt out a single hand on the patchwork quilt. As he did so, he wondered what was happening in Mahanoy City.

At that moment in Mahanoy City, William M. Thomas lay writhing in the street by the breaker. Two bullet holes were in his chest and another in his leg. Two men had fired at close range, another from ambush. A fat housewife, shaking out her rugs, had seen them dashing for the hills. Three of them, she thought. Perhaps she could describe them. Hard to say. They was Irish, though, the lot of them.

They raced madly through the surrounding forests, skipping along the edge of roads, splashing through tiny streams. Their throats were dry and their chests heaving. They were frightened but strangely elated. The deed had been done and so they reported proudly to Kehoe that evening at Carroll's. He seemed unimpressed, distracted.

"Shot and killed him, did you?"

"We did so." Gibbons who replied looked to the others for confirmation. Their heads bobbed affirmatively. "I hit him twice meself, I think."

Kehoe stared at his own gnarled hands, cracked the knuckles once. "Well, Bill Thomas ain't dead yet. What's more, the doctors think he'll live. You bungled it." He rapped the table angrily.

"But we was as close to him as to yourself. We fired right into him."

Kehoe shrugged. "He's alive is what I'm tellin' you. And he may know who done it."

"He don't know us, Jack. Never seen us before. Sure, we had to have him pointed out by McKenna a week ago."

Kehoe swung around to face them. His chair groaned, matching his mood. "Ah, you're a stupid lot. If your brains was dynamite, you'd not have enough to blow your nose. If he sees you again, he'll spot you right enough. And where was McKenna anyway? This was his job."

Hurley explained. "He was sick in bed. A fever."

"You seen him?"

Hurley nodded. "Seen him and talked to him. Then I stuck with him like you said. Played cards by his bed all mornin' while he snored away.

"He didn't leave, then? And no one come to see him?"

Carroll interrupted. "What's this all about, Jack? Red McKenna's as good a man as any of us. What's this watchin' him like a blackleg spy?"

Kehoe stood up and set his empty glass on the bar. Then he turned and rested his elbows on the counter as he spoke. "Ed Kelley was arrested today in Tamaqua. And Alex Campbell picked up at Summit Hill. And there's a warrant out for Tom Munley chargin' him with the shootin' of Sanger and Uren."

For a moment there was stunned silence. Then Carroll spoke again, "But what has this to do with McKenna?"

"I don't know," said Kehoe, "but I'll tell you something else."

"What's that?"

"I was up in Catawissa two days ago. Seen the body master there."

"So?"

Kehoe proceeded slowly, deliberately. "There's been no police there for weeks. Nothing but a couple of watchmen. Old men. McKenna lied to us." His eyes narrowed as he repeated the charge. "He lied to us all."

TEN

A Sudden Farewell

*A*fter two days in bed, Red McKenna returned to work. A crisp breakfast, a few minutes in the autumn air, and then he and Captain Mike were crawling through the familiar tunnel. His own breath was harsh in his ear but he felt strong after the layoff.

"Enjoy your vacation?" an old-timer asked him, then squealed in laughter.

"I'd have been longer, surely," replied Red, "but I missed you all."

Again the good-natured chuckle. And at the face there was more joking, more laughter. Except for John Gibbons, who glared briefly at Red, his eyes burning out of his black countenance, McKenna caught the look and wondered about it. He turned again but Gibbons was assaulting the vein of coal with his pick, fiercely, like a man trying to work off anger. Red shrugged, but the thought stayed with him as he dug into the mound of coal. All morning the picks smashed with a hollow crack and Red scraped and scooped, filling two mule carts. At noon they broke for a bit of lunch.

Mike edged closer to his younger companion. "You in some kind of trouble, Red?"

Red paused, a piece of bread between his fingers. "Why, no. Why'd you ask?"

"No particular reason. Thought I read the signs—knowin' you and knowin' a few other things. You're sure now?"

"Sure as the mornin' sun."

Mike nodded, unconvinced, but they returned to work, slugging away at the ebony wall, biting into it, inch by inch.

♣

That night there was a special meeting called in the back of Carroll's Saloon. Jack Kehoe was there—and Roarity, Kerrigan, Jimmy Boyle, and those who had gone to Mahanoy City. Red McKenna was deliberately excluded.

"Four more arrested in Centralia today," Kehoe began. "Pat Hester, Tom Donahue, Michael Prior, and Jack Duffy. You know some of them yourselves. They're in on a charge near ten years old. You remember the killin' of Rea, the mine super? Them same four was acquitted once, ten years ago, but they have 'em again. Hester's a good man. They're all good men." He glowered at the others, challenging them somehow to live up to the prisoners.

Hugh McGehan—blunt, rugged, craving action—clenched his fists. "What do we do about it? What can we do?"

Kehoe chose his words carefully. "We must kill Red McKenna—if that's his real name at all—before he hangs half the people in Schuylkill County."

Carroll shook his head. "I can't believe it. What makes you sure he's behind this? He's been with us months. He comes recommended."

"Recommended by himself! What do we know about him? Only what he told us—about the shooting in Buffalo and that stuff about the army pension."

"Whippin' Bully Frazier was no fluke. I seen it myself. And he works as hard as any."

"Oh, he's a dandy scrapper, and he's supposed to work hard. That's the scheme of it."

Carroll cocked his head inquisitively. "What are you drivin' at, Jack Kehoe?"

"I got it pretty straight he's a Pinkerton detective. He come here as a labor spy. That's why he works hard and makes friends easy like. It's his job."

"Impossible." Carroll muttered it almost to himself.

"Is it? You'll wish it when he comes swoopin' down here with the blacklegs and we all end in the clink or dancin' on a rope. I'm still givin' the orders and I say he goes."

Kerrigan smiled. He never cared for Red McKenna. "How's it to be?"

"One man can do it." Kehoe shifted his gaze to Jimmy Boyle. "And you're that man, Jimmy. I've heard tell you've no love for him anyway."

Jimmy stood up. "Count me out on that."

"You've been counted in." There was a threat in Kehoe's voice.

Jimmy was equally determined. "Then count me out again. I don't like the man, that's true, and he may be all you say he is, but I'll not have his blood on my hands. Even if you be right, Jack Kehoe, I'll not go through with it." He made no move to leave, merely waited with arms folded.

Kehoe cursed aloud and addressed himself to Jimmy. "All

right, we'll count you out. Out of this job and out of the Order. We'll handle McKenna another way."

Jimmy turned toward the door.

Kehoe checked him. "Not yet, Jimmy Boyle. One last word. You speak of this to anyone and you're marked for next."

"And I'll do *that* job meself," added Kerrigan, grinning.

Jimmy faced them both momentarily, then spun on his heel and left.

"Shouldn't we follow him?" Kerrigan asked.

Kehoe shook his head. "Although he won't do the deed himself, I'm thinkin' he'd like to see it done. Then Kitty Flannery would have no choice but himself. He'll be quiet."

They rearranged their chairs and began the meeting anew. Every face was murderous in the lamp's yellow light, every eye intense. A plan was drafted and hands clasped in token of secrecy. Then they left the room and ordered a round of drinks.

Jimmy Boyle had started for the rig which would take him home, then paused and walked almost automatically toward West Patch. In a few minutes he was standing in the shadows across from the Flannery's house. Many times he had stood there after bidding Kitty a long good-night, and he'd see the lights grow dim and imagine her there kneeling in prayer or perhaps dreaming of him. No more. Now the lights were on and people were moving about and he was not among them.

"I'm a fool," he told himself. "Suppose he's killed? What's it to me? It would be the same with Kitty and me again and me sore lonely now without her." Yet he knew it would never be the same and this troubled him. "Let him worry about himself," he continued, in silent argument. "If I talk, it could be me own back feelin' them bullets. Who's to know?"

He saw Sean at the window, parting the curtains and staring out into the night. As he slid behind a tree, his pulse quickened. He glimpsed Kitty in the lamp-lit background. He couldn't forget. Even if she could, God help him, he couldn't. For several minutes he merely leaned against the tree, thinking, and then he sighed so audibly as to startle himself. Reaching into his pocket, he extracted the stub of a pencil and then probed again until he came up with a cigarette paper. Scribbling a few words on the scrap, he folded it and wrote Red McKenna's name on the outside.

The curtain was drawn now as he crept up to the Flannery porch, trembling with the thought of discovery. He slid the note beneath the door, rapped once, and darted away. When Captain Mike opened the door, he could only squint into an empty yard and listen to the echo of fading footsteps. Stooping, he picked up the tiny note.

"For you," he said, handing it unopened to Red McKenna. Red forced a smile. "Sure, the postman's late today. I hope it's nothin' wrong with the president in Washington or the governor there in Harrisburg. Excuse me." He parted the note like a book and read it, feeling Mike's eyes on him.

"You're discovered," the note read. "They mean to kill you." He kept on smiling as he crumpled it and buried it in his pocket.

"No trouble, I hope," said Bridget, setting down her mending.

Red laughed. "Just a joke, but not for the ears of ladies. Some of the boys wonderin' why I'm not there for cards. Funny humor they have, indeed." He laughed again.

"Aye," said Mike evenly, "they're a gay group, it's true." Red glanced at him, couldn't face his quizzical gaze and turned back to Bridget.

"Where was we? You were tellin' me about the time you scalded the old cat with the cabbage water." Red grinned uncomfortably but Bridget continued, believing that the note was merely a joke. He felt the paper against his thigh, warning him, and he felt Mike's piercing eyes studying his mood. He shifted uneasily but the moment passed.

The night passed, too, and in the morning Red McKenna awoke with a feeling of anxiety. What was behind the note, he wondered? What had prompted its delivery? And by whom?

In his cheerful attitude, however, Mike and Sean read none of the wariness or determination that now marked their companion. He reported with them as usual, did his typical stint at the end of the shovel, joshed with the other miners and emerged from the pit smiling and apparently carefree. Not all of the miners smiled in return and Red noticed this, figuring them for conspirators or, at least, as aware of the conspiracy.

"Why don't you run along, Mike—you and Sean? I'll be with you later," Red remarked as they left the mine shack. "Don't hold supper for me."

Again Mike regarded him closely but merely said, "All right. Be careful." It was a comment that might have been dropped innocently but Red probed for a deeper meaning. Mike's expressionless face told him nothing, so he walked off, straight toward Carroll's Saloon.

Besides Carroll, Kerrigan and Roarity were there, engaged in their endless game of poker. Hugh McGehan was handwrestling across a table with another husky miner. Red's entrance brought all activity to a temporary standstill. Then it started again, like a watch rewound. As Red approached Roarity's table, the players tossed in their cards and waited for Red to speak.

"Might as well be direct," Red began. "I hear there's rumors about me not bein' level with ye. Some say . . ."

"Where'd you hear that?" Kerrigan interrupted.

"No matter. I heard it and I come to have it out. Every man in the Order gets a trial and that's what I want. A fair trial to clear me name."

Kerrigan wasn't listening. Instead, he spat savagely, missing the spitoon. "Jimmy Boyle's the lad, I'll wager. He has the big mouth about him."

Red cloaked his surprise. Of course, it would be Jimmy. But why?

"Shut up, Powder Keg," ordered Carroll. "You'll get a trial, Red, but not here, not now."

"Where and when, then?" Red leaned toward him in challenge. "You name it and McKenna will be there."

The three men exchanged glances, then Carroll spoke. "You know McAndrew's house—in Shenandoah, north of town, past the fork?"

Red shook his head.

"Well, you know the fork?"

"I do so."

"Come there and we'll have someone meet you so there's no slip. What about Saturday night, just past eight?"

Red pressed for a speedy solution. "What about tomorrow—same time?"

Again the furtive looks and, finally, Carroll agreed. "To-morrow night. Eight o'clock. Someone will be at the fork."

Red nodded, looked from one face to the other, and then, in jocular fashion, said, "Goodnight, now, and pleasant dreams to the lot of ye." Bowing, he turned and disappeared out the swinging doors.

The next day it snowed, not much, but enough to cover the ground. It was early and old-timers talked of a long winter and hunger in every home. Brendan said an early snow meant young men would die. As the arrests mounted, this prediction was easy to credit.

Red McKenna shuffled through the snow, wrapped in a yellow slicker which kept out the flakes but not the biting chill. The livery stable was across the railroad tracks and Red intended to borrow a rig for the Shenandoah journey. Once again he had excused himself from supper and aroused Mike's suspicions.

As he neared the squat, dirty station house, his keen eyes made out the forms of several men lounging nearby, pick handles, axes, and mine sledges in their hands. Others might be inside. Thus far they hadn't seen him. He stepped into a doorway to reconsider and while he waited he spotted Sean returning from an errand with a sack of meal in his arms.

"Sean!" He signaled, and Sean responded to his summons.

"Sean, lad, could you do me a favor and no questions asked?"

"Why, sure, Red." The boy was puzzled.

"Good lad. Here's a dollar. Do you go now to Clarity's stable for the loan of a rig. Tell him nothing except you'll have it back this same night. Go quickly now." He shoved Sean gently into the street. The boy looked back once and then crossed the tracks, returning in fifteen minutes with the horse and shay.

Red thanked him. "You're me own sweet darlin'. Not a word of this to the folks, you hear." He held a finger to his lips. "Our secret."

Sean nodded, frowning. He stood in the street as Red whipped the sprightly mare, clucked to her, and then leaned forward for the dash across the tracks. The shay bucked as they bounced over the rails, nearly spilling McKenna. A few men darted out of the darkness but they could only glare after the departing vehicle. Sean saw them and wondered. Then, feeling the cold flakes dissolving on his neck, he started for home, turning several times the first hundred yards to stare after the shay as it vanished in the light snowfall.

Red McKenna covered the ten miles in less than an hour and reined in at the Shenandoah fork. Snow dusted across the carriage and his horse snorted and shook her head. No one seemed to be around. Suddenly a man stepped from behind a tree and placed his hand on the bridle. Red recognized him as Edward Sweeney, a young, balding miner from Mauch Chunk with large teeth that protruded beyond his lower lip. His smile was more of a grimace.

"The nights are very dark," said Sweeney, using the Order's challenge.

"I hope they will soon mend," Red responded.

"I'm to take you in," Sweeney explained. "You'd best leave the rig here."

Red nodded, secured the mare, and then joined his guide. There were few lights in town and even these were clouded in white mist. McKenna drew his collar tighter and shivered involuntarily. Again the pitiful smile from Sweeney. They scuffed along in silence, their feet spraying snow. All about them were the white hills laced with shadows of maples and elms. Stores were closed; the mine shut down. From a distant bar came the tinkling sound of a piano, the rattle of glasses. Red noticed Sweeney dropping a bit behind. First by half a step, then a step, now almost two paces. Red pretended to stumble and called out, "Sure, I'm not familiar with this route at all. There be holes all over and the snow's in me eyes. Would you be good enough to walk on ahead?" He made a sweeping, cavalier gesture with his arm.

Sweeney hesitated, then stepped in front, his hands thrust deep in his pockets. Red followed closely, alert and wary. As they neared the McAndrews' house, Red was aware once again of movement in the vicinity. That would be men outside the house, he thought. No lights showed through the windows.

"Sure, McAndrews must be an owl," Red said jokingly. "Else he's forgotten he's got company."

Sweeney stared at him strangely, not smiling at all. He opened the gate for Red. "You first," McKenna directed, following Sweeney through the gate, across the yard, and onto the porch. Boards creaked beneath his feet and he noticed footprints—a lot of them—radiating out from the porch. Quickly he turned over in his mind the possibility of ambush and he plotted his escape route. The door swung open and he found himself ushered into a dark hallway. Sweeney closed the door behind him, leaving McKenna alone.

"This way," a voice directed. He marked it as Kehoe's and was not surprised. In pursuit of the sound, he stumbled into a larger room, where the outlines of seated figures were dimly visible. He could not tell how many there were nor who they were. No one spoke.

Red reacted to the silence. "I'm here for the trial and, since I've a rented rig and work in the mornin', let's have it over."

"There's to be no trial." It was Kehoe's voice, dull and ominous.

Again Red considered the possibility of escape. Not through the front yard, surely, for there were men hiding out there. He tapped his teeth with a fingernail, rapidly, then spoke again. "And why is there to be no trial? It's in the laws of the Order."

He heard Kehoe shift in his chair but the others were as immobile as statues. "There's no need for a trial, Red McKenna. I'm that sure you're guilty."

"And of what, may I ask?"

Kehoe's voice was soft, menacing. He spat out the words. "You're a detective sent here to spy on us. Deny it now if you will."

Cautiously, Red replied to the charge. "What are you trying to pull, Kehoe? Where did you hear such nonsense?"

"There's a conductor on the Reading line first told me. Then . . ."

Red interrupted. "He's a liar and I'll prove him so!"

Again the dull, abusive tone. "And Father McDermott, too. You'll prove him a liar, I suppose? He knows you for what you are."

Red's voice shook ever so little. "I'll see him on that. I'll see him tonight."

"You do that."

"Yet tonight I'll see him. I'll get the clean bill."

"You do that." Kehoe repeated himself and then fell silent. Red took this as dismissal and, drawing a deep breath, he turned his back on the assembly and groped for the door. Once in the hallway, he moved toward the back of the house, edging along the wall, leaving by the rear door. No one was there but he spotted a man pressed against the wall and facing away from him. Retreating across the backyard, he dropped into a drainage ditch and hunched along, out of sight. Scarcely a quarter of a mile away, he ran into swampy marshland, made cold and soggy by the snow. His feet submerged with each step, bringing a chill to his entire body. But he plodded along, his teeth chattering and his face dripping sweat. Soon he turned from the swamp, clambered up the bank and circled back to his rig. Through the bushes he spied the impatient mare pawing the white surface of the road. No one seemed to be around. He decided to take a chance. From his place of concealment, he dashed to the carriage, vaulted into the seat, and jerked the startled animal about. Applying the switch vigorously, he soon had the mare pounding back to Pottsville. The road was white before him, the hills fuzzy and indistinct. His ears picked up the sound of other hoofbeats blending with those of his own mare. Turning, he saw that he was not alone. A buckboard, with two men astride the front seat, was churning down the narrow lane. A coincidence, perhaps, but Red felt he could take no chances. He hollered to the mare, coaxing speed out of her, and snapped the thin whip above her head. On they plunged in the swirling darkness.

Once they reached the hills, the pace slowed. Red could hear the mare straining, snorting. Her feet slipped as they clattered around the winding curves. The other rig gained. He could hear the pursuers shouting, hear the crack of their buggy whip. They'd have him within a couple of miles. Taking the reins, he wrapped them around the carriage post, then reached under his coat and withdrew a black revolver. The buggy swept on with the buckboard closing the gap. Red let his horse have her head then leaned back in the rig, resting his pistol against the backboard. Snow stung his eyes and the landscape tilted and reeled as he tried to take aim. The buckboard was less than fifty yards away. He thought he recognized Dowling and Ned Monaghan, two Mollies from Coaldale. Carefully, he squeezed the trigger.

The shot went wild, caroming into the night. But it served its purpose. His trackers reined in and halted. Laying on with his whip, Red outdistanced them again—lost them, in fact. When he reached Pottsville, the mare was exhausted and he was nearly spent himself. He led the horse to her stall and then set out on foot for the priest's house.

It was nearly midnight as he approached Father McDermott's residence, a grim two room frame building across from the church. Red looked around, then knocked loudly. Each rap was like the bite of a pick. He knocked again and saw a light flicker inside. Soon the door creaked open, revealing Father McDermott, lamp in hand, and dressed in a faded bathrobe which was cinched around the middle with a brown cord.

"What is it?" the priest sputtered. "Someone ill?"

"It's Red McKenna, Father. I'd have a word with ye."

"Are you daft, man? And it nearly twelve. Can't it wait the night and I'll see you in the mornin'?"

Red stepped into the bleak rectory, brushing past the priest, and tracking the wet snow onto the rough wooden floor. "It cannot wait, Father. The lot of them are after me and they're sayin' you have the bad word agin me. I'll be knowin' that, Father, before I leave." His soft voice had an edge to it.

Father McDermott pinched the sleep from his eyes and slowly closed the door. He gestured for McKenna to sit across from him at the room's only table and then he set the lamp between them. Leaning back, he waited for Red to speak. But McKenna hesitated. His feet were numb, his limbs chilled, and the somber quarters made him uncomfortable. On the rough wall hung an ebony crucifix, with Christ a dark shadow upon it. There was a calendar with many dates circled, an assortment of unfinished chairs. Through an open door, Red glimpsed the ruffled bed, a white basin, and a cracked water pitcher. He turned to Father McDermott, wondering what kind of man he really was. When he spoke, there was discomfort in his voice and a respect he did not intend to exhibit.

"Jack Kehoe said this very night that you've mistaken me for a detective. It's ruinin' me in the estimation of me fellow citizens. And, since it's not true, I'd be obliged if you'd deny it to them."

"Isn't it true?"

"Didn't I tell you it wasn't?"

Father McDermott never moved, scarcely changed expression. "There's no mistake, James McParlan—for that's your real name and you can't say nay to it. I've not used it with Kehoe or any man but I did warn them to shun your company."

Red banged his fist on the table. "It's a lie, whoever told you! There's no truth in it!"

Calmly, the priest went on. "It's true all right. When first I heard of it, I was skeptical but then I went to Philadelphia and checked it out myself. Oh, it's true as Gospel. James

McParlan—secret operative for Pinkerton—assigned to the Schuylkill coal region and working with other agents hereabouts. You've been with Pinkerton since your saloon burned in Chicago in 1871. The letters you were always writing to your mother were reports to headquarters. The mine work was a pose to get inside the organization. Shall I go on?"

Red shook his head, eyes lowered, studying the ragged seams in the floor. When he looked up again, his mood was dark and subdued. "I admits the charge, Father. I'm McParlan and a detective as you've heard. It's a job—like your very own. And I take no money but what's due me, no matter what risk I run."

"I know that."

"Everything from the mine work goes back to the owner. All I get is me agency pay. So there's nothin' in it except doin' me job."

"Who are the others like yourself working in the fields?" asked the priest.

Red shrugged. "I don't know. We have no contact. We're numbers at headquarters, that's all. Can't you see, Father, that we're hired out to see the law upheld?"

Father McDermott arose, turned away from the table, hands clasped behind his back. His gaunt shadow climbed the opposite wall. "You've a lot to answer for, James McParlan. There's men who will die because of you. Innocent men."

"If they're innocent, they'll not die."

"It's a pledge you won't keep—and couldn't, even if you wanted."

Red stroked his chin nervously, then shrugged. "You've told them yourself from the pulpit it was wrong to get mixed up in these killin's. It's justice I'm bringin' to the coalfields. You know it's so, Father."

The priest spun on him. "I do not know it. They'll suffer, I expect, and the courts will call it justice, but I'll withhold judgment. God will judge them—just as He'll judge you, James McParlan."

Red's lips were drawn, his gaze steady. "I hope He'll see I done me duty."

Easing toward him, Father McDermott spoke more sharply, his words cutting McParlan. "Let me say this. Often you knew of these crimes before they were committed. You did nothing to stop them. I ask myself why and the answer comes back that you *wanted* these men to burn and rob and kill."

"Nonsense, Father."

"Is it? You wanted them arrested so you could destroy the union, kill off the leaders. You knew about Jones being shot and about Bill Thomas. You knew of the colliery fires and the secret meetings and God knows how many other things. You could have prevented bloodshed, but you encouraged it."

"I stopped them from blowin' the bridge at Catawissa."

"Certainly, because there was property involved. Property of your employers. But human life is different, isn't it?" Father McDermott was nearly shouting now. "You're lower than them all. They've a name for you, McParlan. A stool pigeon is what you're called. You've turned against them that trusted you."

Angered by the abuse, Red retorted with equal volume. "I told you it's my way of work. How else can they be found out—workin' in the dark like they do? And they deserved it. They surely deserved it."

Father McDermott sat down again, his voice softening after

the outburst. "Perhaps. I did warn them, as you say. I told them that this would be their fate. I should have been stronger, should have forbidden them under pain of sin."

Red gestured sympathetically. "Sure, Father, you did your best."

"Don't lecture me!" the priest roared, slapping the table with his palm. There were tears of anger in his eyes and his face flushed in the amber light. "I should have let them have you. But I haven't lost my wits in the squabble, nor my conscience. Yet these are my people, my responsibility." He paused, hung his head. Behind him, Red had a guilty glimpse of the crucifix. When Father McDermott spoke again, it was merely to say, "There's a train within the hour. You'd best be on it."

Red nodded, shaken by the interview. A man of action, he was not used to doubting himself and this new emotion puzzled him.

Father McDermott interrupted his reverie. "What about the Flannerys? What about Kitty Flannery?"

McParlan looked up, frowning, then turned away. "I—I don't know."

"It was a lie like the rest, I suppose. And convenient living with them to avoid suspicion."

Soberly, McParlan shook his head. "No, Father. In this you must believe me. I was fond of them. I was, truly. And I did love that girl. I do still."

"Had you thought she'd go away with you?"

Red shrugged again. "I hadn't thought that far along. I suppose I hoped . . . I don't know what I hoped."

Again Father McDermott checked him. "No time for these thoughts now. You've less than an hour or I can't answer for your safety."

"Will you see Kitty for me, Father?"

"There'll be no need. Tomorrow the word will be out and it's little enough she'll have to do with you after that."

For a moment, Red considered this, rubbing the heel of his hand along the table edge as he thought. His head bobbed jerkily, affirmatively. "I suppose you're right."

The priest arose, motioned McParlan to his feet, and then blew out the lamp. Stepping to the door, he opened it, and squinted out into the crisp night. The snowfall had ceased and some stars winked ironically. Pottsville was quiet, with only the thin, faraway sounds of the night crews filtering up from the mines.

"I'll not shake hands with you or wish you luck, James McParlan, for then I'd be a hypocrite. You've killed some men here, mind that, and some more will die. It's a spy and renegade you are and not fit for decent company. Go on with you!" The priest's voice was edged with disgust and he tilted his head signaling dismissal.

Red clenched his teeth and accepted the rebuke. Without a word or a backward glance, he stepped into the street. Months ago he had won the town with a song and a smile and with his quick hands and dancing feet. Now he stole away with the idle wind at his heels.

"I'll pray for you," Father McDermott whispered after him.

ELEVEN

The Trials Begin

*T*he old men were right. As the winter moved in, snow stalked it, whirling through the pines and birches, drifting in the streets of Pottsville. In the first storms, the dirty, gray town took on a picture-book quality with the slag piles resembling miniature hills and the wisps of smoke curling up from a hundred black chimneys. Still, there was never enough food and seldom enough warmth. Winter in the Mammoth Vein country had a surface charm that scarcely hid the misery and squalor—like tinsel wrapping on a package of scraps.

Nowhere was there more unhappiness than in the home of Michael Flannery. Coupled with the severe chill of winter was the loss of a trusted friend. Captain Mike was hurt by the deception and Bridget angered in her waspish way.

"Had I the scut here this minute," she declared after his departure, "I'd take the broom to him, front and back, head and heels."

Sean, like his father, was more hurt than angry. First he

had lost his brother and now his closest friend, his idol. For weeks he was unusually quiet and when he finally subdued this mood, he was a changed young man. Deceit and disappointment had entered his life and embittered him. He worked hard, ate sparingly, and he sat alone a great deal, thinking, brooding.

Most of all, of course, the sudden disappearance of James McParlan tormented Kitty. That last night he had come home and quietly packed his things and, just as quietly, had left on the late train. No note, no message, no explanation. She might have forgiven him his role as a detective but she could not forgive this unkindness. At first she wept. Then, stung by the ridicule of her friends, she stiffened in her demeanor, becoming aloof and sensitive. It bothered her that she could still love this man somehow, amid the shame and scorn. As she set about crushing this feeling, she compressed her own personality into a narrow, fruitless entity, like a vein petered out. She had never been more lonely.

Another blow fell. Jimmy Boyle was arrested for the murder of Benjamin Yost. Along with James Carroll, Hugh McGehan, Thomas Duffy, and James Roarity, he was imprisoned in Pottsville and charged with the unsolved crime. Kerrigan, picked up a few days earlier for the shooting of John P. Jones, named Jimmy in his testimony.

"Why would he do that, Brendan?" Captain Mike asked his friend. "Why?"

"That black rogue needs no reason," said Brendan, glowering. "To save his own neck, perhaps, although some say it's because Jimmy gave the warnin' to Red McKenna, or McParlan, or whoever he was.

Mike nodded. "That's likely. And the waste of it. He should have let them have him, I suppose, and he'd be out of it. But, then, I expect he'll be set free anyway once he comes to trial."

Brendan shook his head. "I'd not be sure of it. This is Franklin B. Gowen's big chance to smash the unions. He's roundin' up all the leaders and gatherin' a staff of city lawyers to put them away. You seen any of the papers? They tell me they're cryin' for him to be hangin' the lot of them. No, I wouldn't count on Jimmy Boyle gettin' off. Franklin B. will rant and shout 'til he has them swingin' ropes from the trees."

Mike shook his head. "I hope you're wrong."

Franklin B. Gowen, president of the Philadelphia and Reading Railroad Company, was an implacable foe of labor. Other owners clustered around him, fascinated by his force and his rhetoric. Gowen, a lawyer and former District Attorney in Schuylkill, had rare histrionic skills and enjoyed the public spotlight. It was often charged that he called Stockholders' meetings merely to form an audience for his powerful oratory and to drink in the ensuing applause. Still, he had courage and daring and he was shrewd. Postwar labor troubles and some poor investments made his position shaky. He reckoned that destruction of the Molly Maguires would reinstate him in the good graces of his stockholders. Realizing that convictions would be difficult to get and evidence hard to obtain, he hit upon employing the Pinkerton Detective Agency. In order to retain sufficient glory for himself, he told very few people about this project and maintained direct contact with McParlan.

A man barely forty, Gowen was physically imposing and had a strident voice flavored with a colorful vocabulary. The son of an Irish immigrant and a Philadelphia woman of English descent, he tried unsuccessfully to operate a mine after graduating from college. Turning to the law, he became an attorney and ultimately retained the Philadelphia and Reading Railroad as one of his clients. Rapid promotions followed and now he not only headed the railroad, but he also owned over seventy-five per cent of the collieries in Schuylkill County. His only real failings were an irritating optimism and a dreamer's inability to match large prospects with current problems. His passion for combating the unions cost him a reputed four million dollars. Now he was in Pottsville, as he said, "to rid the mines of the last vestiges of trade unionism."

Some months passed, however, before judges could be appointed and a jury assembled. A score of men languished in the crude jails as winter harassed them augmented by the torturous promise of trial and conviction. The delay had accomplished one thing for the prosecution. They had been able to marshall their forces, both physically and psychologically. Attention was focused on Pottsville from all parts of the nation and most of it was unsympathetic toward the prisoners. They were not so much on trial as was an entire system. Every Irish miner sat in the dock with them. By this public exposé the mine owners hoped to indict all labor and wipe out effective opposition. Motives varied—some selfish and some sincere—but the goals were identical. The Molly Maguires, The Ancient Order of Hibernians, the mine unions—all must be smashed.

Each morning, however, the men went to the mines. They passed the armed squads of Coal and Iron Police and the long file of National Guardsmen who were brought in to keep order. Several detachments encircled the squat, dingy courthouse where the first trial was in session. Michael Doyle,

Edward Kelley, and Alexander Campbell were charged with the murder of mine superintendent John P. Jones. From the privacy of his railroad car, Franklin B. Gowen kept track of the proceedings but he did not enter the courtroom. Instead, one of his colleagues, General Charles Albright, appeared as an aide to the prosecution. In order to call attention to the draft riots among the Irish during the Civil War, the general was in full uniform. He hoped the ribbons and gold braid would remind the jurors of their patriotic duty.

It was cold and drafty in the courtroom as the witnesses—some 120 of them—paraded to the stand. Among them was Jimmy Kerrigan, who had turned State's evidence and now accused his former comrades of the crime.

In an impassioned speech, General Albright made an appeal to the jury—principally farmers—in terms of the financial market provided by the operators. He praised the Coal and Iron Police as "defenders of the law against renegades" and he hinted that acquittal would mean mob lynching anyway.

His prompting was unnecessary. After a long night of discussion and debate, the jury found the defendants guilty of murder in the first degree. This verdict was applauded in the press, the courage of the jurors commended, and the wish expressed that the other trials could be concluded as swiftly and successfully.

In the shanties and the patches, however, the reaction was different. Fear turned to anger as little knots of miners gathered in the evening to discuss the trial.

"What kind of witnesses do you call them?" Brendan was shouting. "Wyhemmer says he seen Kelley pull himself through the bushes after the shootin' and there's no bushes there at all."

Another grizzled miner nodded. "The same with that other one—Belsner, I think. Says he seen a gold button on Eddie's coat seventy-five yards away and then he says he don't even see the flash of the pistol."

"Sure," interjected another, "didn't he point out Kelley's brother in the courtroom and not Kelley himself?"

"It's Kerrigan's the worst of the lot," Brendan said, turning slightly toward Captain Mike who stood by, sucking on his pipe and saying nothing. "Mike, this one swears on the Book he led Kelley and Doyle to Jones in Tamaqua in return for five dollars for whiskey and a ticket home."

"There's some men been sold out for less," Mike responded absently. "James Kerrigan will pay for his lies—if they be lies."

"Of course they're lies. There's no truth in him. Didn't he put the word on young Jimmy Boyle?"

Mike looked up sharply. "Jimmy's not been tried yet. There'll be justice done him, I'm sure of it."

Brendan snorted. "Do you know what Justice is? It's a blind colleen with scales in her hand. One holds a lump of gold and the other a chunk of coal. Which weighs most, do you think?"

The other miners nodded in agreement but Mike pulled on his pipe and replied, "I see Justice as God looking down on the universe, knowing everything, rewarding the good and punishing the wicked. And I see men acting likewise based on the same principles."

"You're looking at it through a penny catechism, Mike. I'm seein' it from a mine shaft. Still, I hope you're right."

They were standing in the roadway, illumined by the moon. Strips of snow lay in the woods and abstract white fragments filled the low places in the fields. The air was chill and vapor floated up with every spoken word.

"Jimmy's trial is next, they say," Brendan reminded Mike, "and they say it will go bad with him."

"I can't believe it will end like that. I just can't believe it."

Brendan touched him on the arm. "It's that you don't want to believe it, Mike."

Mike looked at him soberly for a few seconds before turning away toward the lonely comfort of his home.

TWELVE

The Yost Trial

*I*n the spring, Sean went to work in the mines for the first time. Behind him forever were the long years at the breaker. Another young face took its place opposite Brendan. "Sean," said the old man, reflecting on his own career, "I hope I'll not be seein' you here again."

"You won't, never fear," Sean replied. Then he swung his shovel to his shoulder and disappeared underground in the tracks of his father.

This was May and Jimmy Boyle's trial, scheduled for the first week, was postponed by the death of a juror. It was July before another jury could be impaneled. By that time, Sean Flannery was an experienced laborer, hardened to his task and performing as well for his father as had the others before him. They never spoke of Niall now, nor of Red McKenna. It was one black day following the other, with the heat settling on their tired bodies, bathing them in sweat and dragging their breath out in gasps.

Even above the earth it was torrid and the spectators flocking to the Yost trial wore shirt-sleeves and fanned themselves with newspapers. In the small courtroom, they squirmed uncomfortably. Outside the solid brick structure, national guardsmen stood watch, their bayonets winking yellow in the bright sun. The entire anthracite region was, in effect, under martial law and troops and police were used not only to keep order but, as some suspected, to terrorize witnesses, awe the miners, and intimidate jurors. Across the street, miners' wives perched themselves on porches or plank sidewalks to jeer at the soldiers.

Not all the rancor was in the street. Miners seated in the audience stared at the bench with a mixture of fear and fury. Police ringed the stuffy room, leaning against the cracked plaster with folded arms but not taking their eyes from the miners. Captain Mike sat among them, patiently awaiting the trial and speaking to no one. Unaccountably, he felt drawn to the courtroom and, in order to get away, he had loosened enough coal to keep Sean busy for a few days on his own. As he sat there, he noticed the symbolic scales above the judges' bench and he remembered Brendan's remark, "Coal in one and gold in the other."

There was a stir among the spectators as the trio of judges—Pershing, Green, and Walker—ascended the platform, their faded robes trailing soot from the rude floor. At the sharp rap of the gavel, the crowd scrambled to its feet, then settled down again.

The jurors followed soon after as the clerk read off their names. "Bedford, Brownmiller, Jolly, English, Cake, Libby, Seiders . . ."

"Not an Irishman among them, you can bet," whispered a man behind Mike. "And no Catholics."

His companion replied, "Sure, I know most of them by name. They're all from round about here."

". . . Sterner, Fiddler, Grimm, Cooper, Brennemann," the clerk intoned.

Most of the jurors were farmers. Some were tradesmen or shopkeepers. All of them appeared pale and nervous, perhaps frightened. Rumor cited pressure on the jurors by the owners' vigilance committees.

When Franklin B. Gowen sauntered in, there was another stir. A pace behind him marched General Charles Albright, trim and correct in his blue uniform. Mike's eyes darted over the gold epaulets, the jangling rows of decorations. He examined the proud, haughty face of Gowen as the mine-owner cast an indifferent glance over the audience. A quartet of lawyers, including George Kaerscher and F. W. Hughes, the youthful district attorney, completed the parade.

Defense Attorney James Ryon, formerly president-judge of Schuylkill County, walked in slowly, followed by an assistant named L'Velle and two partners, Linn Bartholomew and J. B. Reilly. Ryon was experienced, quick-witted, alert. He dropped casually into his chair in front of the raised dock. His back was to the defendants as they filed in.

Roarity came first, looking unkempt and defiant. Then James Carroll, serious as usual, but outwardly calm. Jimmy Boyle, too, was calm and impassive. Only Hugh McGehan, his mouth agape and his rugged hands clenching and unclenching—only Hugh looked troubled and bewildered. Thomas Duffy had asked for—and received—permission for a separate trial.

Judge Pershing rapped again for order. Already he was

perspiring in his heavy robes and he swabbed his eyes and forehead with a wrinkled kerchief.

The attorneys were introduced, then the prisoners called by name. Mike stared hard at Jimmy Boyle, trying to read his feelings, but Jimmy's gaze wandered absently about the courtroom, seeing no one.

As the first prosecution witness, Mrs. Benjamin Yost was called to the stand. The policeman's wife repeated the death-bed statement of her husband. General Albright drew the testimony from her patiently and, although she stumbled over the English, her story was credible and sincere.

"What was the time again, Mrs. Yost? You said 2:30 in the morning, I believe?"

"Ja. That's right." The widow nodded and her eyes were wide. "He was almost finished outing the lights."

"And then you saw these men . . ."

"No. Only the flash of the guns."

"But your husband saw them."

"Ja."

"Did he name them?"

The frightened woman shook her head. "No. It was dark. He could not see them."

"What did he say about them?"

"He said they were two Irishmen, one smaller than the other."

"Thank you." General Albright smiled and sat down, clearing the way for Ryon's cross-examination. The defense attorney shuffled to the witness stand.

"Mrs. Yost, do you, yourself, recognize any of the defendants seated there?" He stabbed a bony finger at the dock.

She shook her head slightly. "Are they Irishmen?"

"I believe they are.

"Do you see any other Irishmen in this room?"

She looked at him quizzically and nodded again. "Ja. There are many."

"Could you pick them all out?"

"I . . . I don't know."

"Could you pick them out in the darkness at 2:30 in the morning?" Ryon's voice was rising. "Could you see they were Irishmen?"

General Albright jumped to his feet, medals clinking. "I object to this line of questioning, your honor. Mrs. Yost is not on trial. She merely repeated her husband's statement."

"Sustained." A bead of sweat rolled down the judge's nose.

Ryon bowed slightly in submission, then turned again to Mrs. Yost. "Did you speak to your husband in English, Mrs. Yost?"

"No, in German."

"No one else heard this deathbed conversation, then?"

"The doctor only."

"Thank you. No more questions." Ryon helped her down from the stand.

Captain Mike watched soberly as a succession of witnesses were brought forth by the prosecution. Some related specific facts; some made general accusations. Attorney James Ryon challenged all of them.

"Mr. Brislin," remarked the defense attorney to one witness, "you relate having seen the defendants, Hugh McGehan and James Boyle, on the day of the murder, hurrying through the woods past your house."

"That's correct, sir."

"And where were you?"

"Inside my house."

"But Mr. Brislin, the path is a hundred yards in front of your cottage. If these men were running—and at that distance—how could you distinguish them?"

"I know what I seen."

Albright started to object but Ryon waved him away and changed the line of questioning.

"You are employed, Mr. Brislin, by the Lehigh and Wilkes-Barre Coal Company?"

"I am."

"Have you not been promised a promotion? To mine boss, to be specific?" Ryon leaned toward the witness, his hand on the arm of the chair.

Brislin swallowed hard, darted a glance at Gowen. "I have, but..."

Ryon's voice became louder, more cutting. "Wasn't this promise made before this trial, Mr. Robert Brislin? Wasn't it made depending on your testimony at this trial? Wasn't it?"

"No, no." Brislin shifted in his seat.

"It wasn't made before the trial then?"

"Well, yes, but..."

The defense attorney turned his back on him. "That's all."

When Mrs. Burns, Hugh McGehan's landlady, took the stand, he badgered her in a similar fashion.

"You've told the general, Mrs. Burns, and the gentlemen of the jury, that your boarder, Hugh McGehan, came home late that night and told you he'd been at Summit Hill and Nesquehoning. Is that right?"

Mrs. Burns was a round, pudgy woman, her cheeks heavily

rouged, her clothes tight and comically gaudy. "That's right, sir." She smiled at the jury.

Ryon did not smile. "Now, Mrs. Burns, why is it you told the authorities at the inquest in May that Mr. McGehan had been home all night?"

There was a pause and then Mrs. Burns smiled again, this time with less amusement. "I lied then."

"But you're telling the truth now?"

"I am. The priest told me I should tell the truth."

"What priest?"

"I'll not tell you that. Sure, it's a matter of me own confession."

Ryon sighed and dismissed her.

Franklin Gowen took the next witness. In his polished manner he queried an aging gunsmith named E. B. Whitenight.

"You recognize this pistol?" Gowen held up a dark revolver, purported to be the murder weapon.

"It's one of mine."

"Look at the defendants, now." Gowen indicated the prisoners. "Do you see seated there the man who purchased this pistol?"

Whitenight rubbed a forefinger across his dry lips. His brow furrowed. "I—I don't know. I can't really say."

"You can't say! This is a murder trial, Mr. Whitenight. These men are accused of shooting another human being in cold blood. You *must* say."

The gunsmith turned away from the prisoners in confusion. "All I remember is that he had dark hair."

Gowen whirled toward the jury. "Look there! Look at James Roarity. Note him well. Who has darker hair than he?"

Ryon lifted himself to his feet. "Objection, your honor. That charge is ridiculous. Dozens of men in this room have dark hair—including two members of the jury."

There was laughter at this outburst but Ryon knew the prosecution had scored a point. A stupid, irrelevant point, to be sure, but many trials hung on such trivialities.

A number of character witnesses were summoned by the prosecution. Most of them were honest citizens; a few were paid to lie. Even the most sincere among them were frightened by tales of witnesses who had told the truth only to find themselves imprisoned later on charges of perjury.

A German farmer wrung his cap nervously in two gnarled hands as he testified.

"Have you ever heard that James Carroll was a Molly Maguire?" inquired General Albright.

"Other people used to say he was."

"Is a man who is called a Molly Maguire a man of good character?"

"It is more than I can say. He never done anything to me."

"The question is, is a man called a Molly Maguire a man of good character?"

The farmer evaded the question. "The Germans do not bother about them."

"Do the Germans call Molly Maguires men of good character?"

There was despair in the tone of the witness. "I cannot answer that. I do not know that."

Another man was called, a tailor from Storm Hill. His collar was damp and, as he arose, he dropped the paper with which he was fanning himself. A few windows were opened and were quickly closed when the jeers from the street crowd drowned out the testimony.

"Do you know this defendant, James Boyle?" Gowen asked the tailor.

"I do," the witness replied evenly.

"How long have you known him?"

"I cannot tell exactly. Five, six, seven years, perhaps."

Gowen kept on, quietly, dominantly. "Will you please tell us if you know what has been his reputation in the vicinity where he lives, since you have known him, up to the time of his arrest, for peace, good order, and quiet?"

The tailor answered flatly. "I never heard anything against him."

Gowen was sly. "Have you ever heard he was a Molly Maguire?"

The tailor shrugged. "I have."

"And yet you say you have never heard anything against him?"

"Nothing against him except that." The witness did not realize he had been tricked. Mike groaned inwardly.

Kerrigan was next. Of all the witnesses, his appearance brought out the most antagonism. The overflow crowd jeered, bringing the policemen to attention and evoking a staccato rap from the judge's gavel. Roarity spat and was reprimanded from the bench. Only Kerrigan seemed undisturbed. He told his story straight, mixing half-truths with lies, and declaring upon his oath that what he said was true.

"It was a plot of the Ancient Order of Hibernians—of the Mollies themselves," he said in answer to Gowen's question.

"Are the murderers present in this courtroom?"

Kerrigan smiled slightly. "They are. Hugh McGehan there. And Jimmy Boyle."

"You're sure of that?"

"I seen them myself. They made up the plan in Carroll's place and it was Roarity loaned the pistol for to kill Yost as had once beat him up."

Gowen kept Kerrigan on the stand for forty-five minutes, eliciting from him details of other crimes and drawing a picture of the Molly Maguires in the blackest possible terms.

"I been in a fight with Yost, too," Kerrigan admitted. "Me and Tom Duffy and us drunk at the time. That's why I was in on it all. We was on Carroll's porch there when Duffy says he'd give Roarity ten dollars if he'd shoot Yost and Roarity says he would or, if he couldn't, he'd get two fellows that would."

Roarity leaped to his feet. "You're a lying scut, Kerrigan. There's no truth in it at all. Sure, wasn't I home the whole while with my wife sick."

Again the judge slammed down the gavel and two policemen pulled Roarity back to his stool.

"I helped Roarity get the others together. All of them there." Kerrigan waved his hand at the prisoners. "I wanted out of the deed meself but they wouldn't let me off. I showed them the way to Tamaqua and back again. That's all I done."

In cross-examination, L'Velle assailed the character of the witness. "This is a man who has a reputation as a drunkard, a loafer, a scoundrel, a troublemaker, even a thief and a murderer. He deserted his family and he's turned on his friends."

Gowen objected. "His past is immaterial. It only matters now that Mr. Kerrigan is on the right side."

"The right side, is it? Meaning, I suppose, your side?"

"The side of the law."

"We'll see about that. Your honor, I'd like to call Daniel Schepp to the stand."

Judge Pershing looked toward Gowen. "Does the prosecution have any more witnesses?"

"Only one more, but we'll yield to the defense for the moment, if we have your permission to call our final witness later."

"Granted."

L'Velle questioned Schepp, a friend of Yost, very carefully, though briefly.

"Did the deceased know Kerrigan?"

"He did. He arrested him many times. Maybe half a dozen."

"Did he ever say anything about him?"

Schepp nodded timorously. "He was afraid of him. Him and Duffy. He always put them two together."

There was no cross-examination, so L'Velle called upon Dr. F. S. Solliday who had attended Yost at his death. The doctor corroborated much of the testimony of Mrs. Yost but added these words: 'I heard Yost whisper to Barney McCarron, 'Be careful of Kerrigan. They will have you yet, the same as they have me.'"

Finally, James Ryon introduced Mrs. Kerrigan, a drab and miserable figure, who trembled as she took the stand and swore on the Bible to tell the truth. Ryon paced in a semicircle before her, asking questions slowly, deliberately.

"Was your husband the owner of a pistol?"

"Yes, sir."

"About how long had he owned the pistol?"

"I think about a year."

"What did he do the night he came in—the night of the murder? After you let him in, what did he do?"

Mrs. Kerrigan hung her head, her gray hair falling in wisps about her forehead. "Why, he had his boots in his hand when I let him in, and he said he shot Yost."

A few moments later, Gowen strode forward and plied the woman with questions. She was more composed now and replied with some vigor to his insinuations.

"You've not seen your husband since he's been imprisoned, have you?" Gowen hovered over her.

"No, sir."

"Have you refused to send him clothes?"

"Yes, sir."

"And do anything for him?"

"Yes, sir."

Gowen paused, turned away from her toward the jury, and shot the next question over his shoulder.

"Did you not come to Pottsville voluntarily, of your own will, some time ago to make a statement or affidavit that your husband killed Yost? Did you not do that of your own motive?"

"I made that statement before I came to Pottsville," replied Mrs. Kerrigan sharply.

"You made it before Squire O'Brien?"

"Yes."

"You went there voluntarily?"

"Of my own accord."

"To get your husband hung?"

"To tell the truth."

"To have the father of your children hung?" Gowen had returned to her and his face was not a foot from her own.

"Not when I was telling the truth," she replied without fear.

Gowen changed his attack. "Why did you not send him clothes when he was lying in prison?"

"Why? Because he picked innocent men to suffer for his crime."

"Why did you refuse to go and see him when he sent word he wanted to see you?"

The woman pouted a little, weary of the questioning. "Because any man that does such a crime that he done, why should I turn around then and . . ."

"And what? Go on."

"That is all."

"What crime had he done?"

She let out a deep sigh. "The crime of Yost."

"The murder of Yost?"

"Yes, sir."

Again the judge had to rap for order as the courtroom erupted in excited conversation. Gowen sat down thoughtfully and Mrs. Kerrigan left the stand. Men and women shook her hand as she proceeded, tearfully, to the rear of the room. For the first time, Captain Mike felt hopeful about the outcome. Even Roarity managed a tight smile.

Judge Pershing looked at his watch and at the other judges, then turned to Ryon. "Are there any more defense witnesses?"

"None, your honor; we rest our case."

"Prosecution?"

"We have a final witness, your honor, but the hour is late,"

Gowen smiled. "I'd like to move for adjournment and place my witness first on tomorrow's docket."

"Very well. His name?"

Gowen arose, paused for the dramatic effect. "Detective James McParlan, late of this region."

An audible gasp of surprise filled the room. Mike half rose from his seat. His eyes flicked to Jimmy Boyle but Jimmy displayed no emotion at the news.

"James McParlan, alias Red McKenna," thought Captain Mike. "And he's comin' back to Pottsville!"

THIRTEEN

Red's Homecoming

*E*arly the next morning, a squad of Coal and Iron Police escorted James McParlan from the first train. Oblivious to the taunts and threats that were hurled at him, he strolled up Pottsville's main street. Past the familiar landmarks he walked and past the sullen miners. He wore his derby at a jaunty angle and his light brown suit, wrinkled now from the train ride, was of the latest cut. He skipped up the courthouse steps and into the stuffy anteroom where Franklin B. Gowen awaited him.

"A lively crowd outside," Red remarked. "Nothing like blood to draw the pack, my mother did often say."

Gowen bit the end off his cigar and spit it out. "You made good time," he said, flatly.

"I come fast as I could after gettin' your wire. For a fact, I was surprised you sent for me at all. The bargain was, I was not to testify in court."

"Things change." Gowen lit his cigar and took a long drag, exhaling a cloud of dark smoke. "Things change, McParlan. There's little doubt we'll convict these cutthroats but there's fifteen more of the same Order awaiting trial. We'll try the Molly Maguires here as well as these four buckos."

"I see."

"Do you know what you're to do, McParlan?"

"Yes, sir, I think so. Just to tell all I know about the Mollies and the Ancient Order and the Unions themselves."

Gowen nodded. "Leave nothing out. And make it as authentic as possible."

"Sure, you'll think you lived it yourself."

Another puff of smoke followed. "Now, do you have any questions?"

"Just one. About this Jimmy Boyle. He couldn't have been in on the Yost thing. He joined up same day as I did and that was months after the shootin'. So he's clean of guilt."

"Too late for that. Kerrigan's already implicated him."

"But why?"

Gowen shrugged. "Private reason, I guess. No matter. You'll have to go along."

McParlan stared at him, unbelieving. "But he wasn't there, Mr. Gowen! I'll be sending up an innocent man."

"Perhaps. It may be he was in it all along. How do you know? Kerrigan says he was. And we have to back up Kerrigan. His wife did a lot of damage to our case yesterday. We can't let them pick it apart."

McParlan slumped into a wicker chair, shaking his head. Gowen edged over and put a hand on his shoulder.

"In all great enterprises, there must be some accidents. This is our chance to rid the coalfields of this disease and we can't let it collapse on a probability. It's true that Jimmy Boyle was a Molly Maguire—before or after the fact—and that's good enough for me."

"Yes, sir." Red agreed without enthusiasm.

When he entered the courtroom, he had regained his composure. Unlike Kerrigan, he was not timid about facing his former companions—except for Jimmy Boyle, whom he knew he must wrong.

"Your name, please?" It was the clerk of court calling him back to reality.

"James McParlan."

"Are you the same James McParlan that lived and worked in Pottsville, Tower City, Port Clinton, and elsewhere under the name of James McKenna?"

"I am."

Gowen took over, facing the jury. "The prosecution proposes to prove by James McParlan, the witness on the stand, that, as a detective officer, he became acquainted with the four prisoners now on trial in the capacity of a private person, and that three of the prisoners on trial, Hugh McGehan, James Carroll, and James Roarity, confessed to him their participation in the murder of Benjamin F. Yost, both as principals and accessories before the fact, and detailed to him the circumstances attending the commission of the crime, and to prove the confessions thus made to him as evidence against the persons making them."

Ryon objected immediately. "Those confessions were obtained by fraud and not voluntarily and are therefore inadmissible."

"Overruled."

McParlan's testimony was long and replete with specifies, covering his activities since his arrival in the Mammoth Vein area. He told of his fights, his plotting, even the particulars of his induction into the Molly Maguires. In large measure, his evidence paralleled that of Kerrigan, except that it indicted an entire organization rather than a quartet of prisoners.

Midway in the interrogation, General Albright relieved Gowen and pursued the same broad line of questioning.

"Did Hugh McGehan say how or through what agency of influence he expected to get men to kill Benjamin Yost?"

"Why, certainly. It was an understood thing."

Once again Ryon stood up. "We object to that question as leading."

"Overruled."

The general continued. "What organization did he say?"

"The Ancient Order of Hibernians, the Molly Maguires."

Judge Pershing leaned over the bench. "He said that, did he?"

The detective shrugged slightly. "He did not say that. But he expected to get help from Schuylkill, of course. We understood from that conversation what was meant. . . ."

"Did he name any particular person, or persons, in connection with the murder?"

"Yes, sir. He named James Roarity as a particular person. And Thomas Duffy."

"And the fourth defendant here?"

"Sir?"

General Albright repeated his question. "And the fourth defendant—James Boyle?"

Red looked up at Jimmy Boyle seated in the dock. Their eyes met for an instant but, in Jimmy's glance, there was no plea, no sign of recognition. Turning quickly to Gowen, Red saw the warning frown and remembered his instructions.

"And Jimmy Boyle." His words could barely be heard.

As the defense attorney began his cross-examination, he

addressed a few remarks to the court. The place was sweltering and Ryon had stripped off his coat and appeared in his shirt-sleeves, his collar open. Captain Mike, still on hand for the climax of the trial, tasted the salt sweat in the corner of his mouth and felt his clothes sticking to the hard chair. A woman fainted and was carried outside.

Clearing his throat noisily, the defense attorney commenced his speech.

"Immediately prior to 1873, while the Miners' and Laborers' Union was in the heyday of its prosperity in this country—I say the Union, and God bless it for the good work it did in this community—there was not a transgression or serious crime in this county for years. When wealth and capital made aggressions upon the rights of the private citizen, what followed? A disintegration of the union; a severing of it; a breaking up of it; and it is undeniable that crime then followed. From 1865 to 1873 there was no such thing as a murder case in Schuylkill County, not until the emissary of death, James McParlan, made his advent into this county. No crime has since been perpetrated except that which he assisted to plot, to counsel, to perpetrate, and to conceal afterward as far as he himself was individually concerned. And why has he done this? I'll tell you why. To discredit the unions and destroy the societies of men. And to make himself a great detective, so he can be given a bureau of his own. You've heard of the great laurels he wears as a detective. If this be true, he wears them while Sanger, and Uren, and John P. Jones, and, yes, Benjamin Yost lie in their graves as his victims."

He paused and there was a scattered burst of applause and a few spontaneous cheers. Once again the gavel brought silence.

"I will tell you how the Pinkerton detective works," continued Ryon. "This mysterious organization, which keeps its records closed to the public, hires special agents for single jobs, general agents for regular work, and for the work of the labor spy they hire secret agents. James McParlan is one of these. He works by a secret number, writes regular reports to a private mailbox and signs them with this number. He works among the men, disorganizes them, spies upon their activities."

Gowen leaped dramatically to his feet.

"We employ spies in wars between nations," he stated. "Is it worse to employ them in wars in society? The Bible tells us, Mr. Ryon, that Joshua concealed spies in the house of Rahab and Saul sent his guards to watch David and Ezechias had spies in the tents of the Assyrians. It is an ancient and a noble practice. The coal region owes this man a debt of gratitude, for he has saved it not only from the crimes which had disgraced it, but from the reign of mob law which would soon have established itself here, to the still greater disgrace of a civilized community. James McParlan is no villain. He is the blood-red wine marked one hundred."

Again there were cheers but, this time, they issued from different throats. Judge Pershing gaveled them down and interjected a few comments of his own.

"The detective system is one which may be greatly abused," he conceded, "but it is only correct to point out that Mr. McParlan never received any compensation beyond the twelve dollars which was his weekly salary. This should be considered in weighing his testimony—this, and to what extent he has contradicted himself and the testimony of others."

But James McParlan never contradicted himself, except

in minor detail. The defense could not shake him. His story was so credible, so rich in dates and facts, that it could scarcely be doubted. In a few instances, the detective even seemed to make admissions favorable to the defense.

In winding up his interrogation of McParlan, Ryon concentrated on the Molly Maguires themselves.

"There are many organizations, Mr. McParlan, which have passwords and secret signs—the Masons, the Odd-Fellows, and so on. Is there anything wrong with this?"

"No, sir, I don't believe there is."

"Is there anything in the rules of the Ancient Order of Hibernians that indicates immoral or criminal intent?"

"No, not in the rules themselves."

"I asked only about the rules. There is nothing criminal in them, then?"

"No, sir "

Red's wrinkled suit was stained with perspiration and he began to look uncomfortable.

"Mr. McParlan, did you tell your comrades in the Order that you were a Catholic?"

"Yes, sir, I did tell them that, and in doing that I told them the truth. That is one thing I did not deceive them in at all."

Ryon eyed him coolly. "That was not a piece of strategy, as Mr. Gowen calls it? He does not call it a lie, he calls it strategy."

"No, sir."

"Did you know that you could be a member of the Catholic Church and join that society?"

"Yes, sir, I knew that."

"You were a member of that Church?"

"Yes, sir. I am a member of that Church."

"Were you then?"

"I was then when I joined the society and I am now." Carefully, Ryon probed deeper. "Did you go to Communion and the confessional after you joined that society?"

Red paused, then answered loudly. "I never did. It was sacrilegious—the idea of such a thing."

Ryon shifted again to an earlier question. "You were present when many of these crimes were planned—in Pottsville and elsewhere?"

"That is true."

"But you did nothing to prevent them?"

"I talked against some of them."

Ryon moved in, pointing his accusing finger. "But you did not warn the victims. You didn't warn Bill Thomas. You wanted him out of the way, too, or didn't worry about him as long as you got your convictions. You did not tell the proper authorities."

"No, sir, I did not."

"And why not? Why not, Mr. McParlan?"

"I'd have given meself away, surely. My job was to discover what I could. . . ."

Ryon shouted at him. "Given yourself away! And was not human life more important? Wasn't . . ."

General Albright was on his feet voicing an objection.

"This line of questioning has been pursued before, your honor. We have established that Mr. McParlan was a detective working in his line of duty. His motives cannot be impugned."

"Sustained."

Ryon nodded grudgingly and then turned to his chair. "No more questions," he said with a sigh.

General Albright was the first to sum up the case for the prosecution. He stood ramrod straight as he made a frank and open appeal to the property interests of the jurors.

"It is almost inconceivable how this evil society has injured you and every property owner in the coal regions. There is no portion of the country richer than the anthracite region. There are probably a hundred million dollars invested directly or indirectly in Schuylkill County pertaining to the coal business alone, embracing, of course, the railroads and canal, and all built for the purpose of getting the rich treasure underlying the surface of the earth.

"It is a fact that not over one third of the capital so invested in these times receives any remuneration. And when you find these conservative enterprises confronted by a body of men who seek to control the coal mines and who, fancying themselves injured, strike down a mining boss or police officer who endeavored faithfully to discharge his duties, you can see how property, how life, how everything have been imperiled, and how men of families—and who love them, too—become alarmed and feel they dare no longer remain in this region. They leave and give place to inferior men and, in consequence, the business of this particular community was about to be surrendered to lawless and desperate men when, by a train of providences, these murderers and assassins were brought to the front, and some of them are now in *this* front, in your presence, and you are about to pass judgment on them."

District Attorney Hughes, who had spoken little during the trial, made a brief plea to the jurors. "Fraud is the logical outgrowth of Molly Maguireism. That and illegal elections, robbery, murder. If it requires the bold surgery of hanging ten, fifty, or five hundred Molly Maguires at the end of a rope, let us apply the surgery. If it is the only way to save ourselves, let's apply it."

As Franklin B. Gowen ambled forward to present the final word from the prosecution, Mike felt a chill come over him. He could sense the passion that was building up in the courtroom. He could read the verdict in the jurors' faces.

Gowen leaned on the railing of the jury box as he began, softly, to recount the crimes and their results. Once into his speech, he was pacing excitedly in front of the twelve men and gesturing emphatically to punctuate his phrasing.

"The gentlemen tell us that the Ancient Order of Hibernians is a good society; but we try it by its acts. We try it, not by its written declarations or spoken denials, but according to the evidence in this case. By that alone your verdict, as I said before, will not only convict the prisoners of the offense with which they are charged, but in the estimation of the people of this county, and of the whole country, will convict this society so that it will never hereafter lift its head to look man in the face, and above all, never hereafter will a member be able to lift his hand to strike the blow that has so often carried terror to the community, which now looks to us as its last refuge."

Warming to his task, Gowen stepped up the pace and volume of his delivery. "And what was the purpose of this organization? The purpose was to get the benefit of and enjoy the use of the property of others without owning it, and without paying for it. The purpose was to make the business of mining coal in this country a terror and a fear; to secure for the leading men in this society profitable positions, and the control of large operations at every colliery. The purpose was to levy blackmail upon every man engaged in industrial pursuits in this country, so that the owners, under the terror which this organization had acquired, would gladly purchase peace and immunity."

Mike stirred uneasily, seeing the effect the address had upon Gowen's spellbound listeners, and, in particular, on the members of the jury.

"Of what use would capital, or wealth, or industry, or enterprise, or protection amount to, if the administration of the resources of this country and the development of its wealth were intrusted to those who went to do their duty, dogged by the assassin and the murderer, unknowing whether, when they left their homes in the morning, they would not be carried back dead before night?"

He echoed Hughes' plea that the prisoners be hanged so that the country might be rid of their contagion.

"We can stand up before the whole country, and say, 'Now all are safe. Come here with your money. Come here with your enterprises. Come here with your families and make this your residence.'"

Gowen crossed his hands upon his chest and then stretched them toward the jurors.

"I believe I have done my duty. For God's sake, let me beg of you not to shrink from doing yours. Solemn judges of the law and of the facts—august ministers in this temple of justice—robed for sacrifice, I bring before you these prisoners and lay them upon your altar . . . and trembling at the momentous issues involved in your answer, I ask you, will you let them go?"

He said the final few words slowly, pausing between each. Then he stared for a silent moment at the jury and sat down.

The jurors only half-heard the first defense plea. L'Velle begged them to give labor an equal chance. "Do not crush it. Let it not perish under the imperial mandates of capitalism in a free country."

To Attorney James Ryon was left the closing speech. He knew it must be persuasive but somehow he felt depressed, as if the case had been decided already. He realized he must counteract, not only the testimony of McParlan and Kerrigan, and the powerful oratory of Gowen, but also the prejudice which had accumulated against the miners during these past months.

He began quietly. "I have no appeal to make to your passion. If an attempt is made to sway your minds away from the facts upon which you have sworn to try this case, that attempt is not only in pursuance to the oaths you have taken in this case, but is contrary to every precept of law and order. When my learned friend told you he had preserved these men for the sacrifice, he reminded me of those days of English history when tribunals were devised for the purpose of making sacrifice of people charged with crime as a pretense for their destruction. We have, pray God, passed beyond that barbarity."

He ripped into the remarks of Kerrigan and McParlan, assailed their characters, challenged their data. He charged an extensive plot to indict an entire race of people. "Has there been an Irishman upon the stand for the last six months in this county who has not been called a Molly Maguire? Can you distinguish between the witnesses as to who are Molly Maguires and who are not? Every Irishman, so far as I have made my observations, has been classed in the same category, and it has been a sort of moving curse which falls not only upon these men arraigned here but upon every man who has been brought to testify anything in aid of these prisoners. Every man of Irish descent who speaks a word in their behalf is charged with perjury."

He mopped his face with his handkerchief, stuffed it into a rear pocket where it hung limp, like the exhausted spectators. "Let me conclude by begging you—by pleading with you—not to sacrifice these men but to listen to the voice of reason and find them guiltless of this crime. Thank you. The rest is in your hands."

He slid into his chair and put his head wearily on the table. The prisoners stared past him at the jurors filing out. It was 3:20 P.M. They might reach a verdict this evening.

Roarity whispered to Carroll. "I'd give it all up for a chance at Kerrigan. I would surely."

"And wouldn't we all? Him and McParlan, with his singin' and dancin' and whole stack of lies."

Jimmy Boyle propped his head on one hand and seemed unaware of the events surrounding him. But he was praying. It was a confused, awkward, sincere prayer. He asked for his life but, if he could not have this, he asked to understand and accept his punishment. When he looked up, he saw Captain Mike for the first time. There were not fifty yards separating them and he could discern the tears in Mike's eyes. He forced a smile but Mike could not return it. He only shook his head as if to say, "No, Jimmy, it can't happen."

But it did happen. The jury returned at 5:00 P.M. with a verdict of "Guilty" and the judge immediately passed sentence. The prisoners rose to receive it.

"You are to be imprisoned here until the completion of the trials and shall then suffer death by hanging. And may God have mercy on your souls."

There was a sudden hush in the room, like silence in the depths of a mine. Then, as the four men were ushered back to their cells, tears and curses blended with the applause.

In his own cell, Powder Keg Kerrigan learned of the verdict and smiled. For his reward, he received his freedom and left the coalfields forever.

FOURTEEN

Two Old Friends Meet

*T*hat night the news of the trial spread quickly. All Pottsville soon knew of the miners' fate and fear settled once more on the shacks and patches. Miners sat glumly at supper and could not eat. There was little conversation, only a brooding pessimism.

Sean Flannery walked home slowly from the mine. "Jimmy Boyle, a man not much older than myself. Jimmy Boyle's to die." In the darkness he could hear the lonely cry of night birds and the hollow crack of limbs in the forest. Half a mile from West Patch, he passed a shadowy corner of the road where branches reached out menacingly from the sloping shoulder. Three years ago a man had been hung there—Frank Gallagher, a young miner from Mauch Chunk. Since then the place had a haunted reputation and Sean prepared to hustle past.

Suddenly he was startled by a voice calling in a soft brogue. "Sean."

He stopped, not daring to look toward the woods. His eyes widened and his legs felt feathery. Before he could break into a run, the voice called again. "Sean. Over here. It's me. Red."

The fright became anger as Sean turned and peered into the underbrush.

Red's voice sounded strange but with some of the playfulness left. "You'll have to come over here, lad. Should I be seen, there's no tellin' but there'd be another rope about this tree."

Sean moved rapidly into the bushes and found Red squatting in a circle of wild hedges, invisible from the road. He appeared annoyingly calm.

Sean stared down at him. "I should call them out against you."

"You could do that, Sean, but then you'd not know what I have to say. Sit down instead. For old times." He gestured politely with an upturned palm.

Slowly and reluctantly, Sean settled on his haunches opposite McParlan. "Say what you have to say then, for I must be for home."

McParlan grew suddenly sober. "I've no right to stop you this way, Sean, but I must leave Pottsville in an hour. I want you to know I'm sorry for what happened. I wish you'd tell Kitty for me that . . ."

Sean made a movement as if to rise. Disgust distorted his boyish features. Red checked him. "Hear me out." With an impatient sigh, Sean settled back again.

"I'm sorry it was Jimmy Boyle was named. He ought not have gone in with them. He was a fool but I'm sorry about him. I want Kitty should know I had nothing to do with his arrest. I'll take my oath on it."

Sean was glumly silent so Red went on.

"Sean, these men—most of them—are criminals. You must believe this. It was me duty to bring them in. I've done nothing dishonorable, nothing wrong. I want you to believe this. I want Kitty to believe it. We were friends once. We can still be friends."

Sean stood and shook his head sharply. "That day is past. I'll not believe you nor think of you again in friendship."

Red arose to face him. Sean seemed older, wiser. It was a conversation between two men, not a man and a boy.

"Listen to me, Sean."

"I've done listening." Sean's own voice was now on edge. "And if I see you again, Red, I'll be obliged to kill you myself."

McParlan smiled ruefully and Sean mistook it for mockery. He lashed out with his fist, missed, and tumbled to one knee. Expecting to be hit, he threw his arm up defensively. But Red merely looked down at him and shook his head.

"Go on home, Sean Flannery. Go on home." Red turned sadly and disappeared into the woods.

 *FIFTEEN*

The Quick and the Dead

A year elapsed before the sentence was enacted. It was a year of misery and terror for the miners. Wages were down, hours longer, and health and safety conditions worse. Any protest was dealt with swiftly and cruelly. Mere membership in the Ancient Order of Hibernians became sufficient for conviction. Other trials followed the Yost trial. Other prisoners left the dock with the verdict of "Guilty" ringing in their ears. For some, this meant a crippling fine or a long jail term. For nineteen men, it meant death. On June 21, 1877, Pottsville witnessed the first execution.

In the hills the streams ran full and the summer sun, hot and bright, reflected in the vacant store windows. Business was suspended for the day, even in the mines. Just to be on the safe side, the saloons, too, were closed until after the hangings. Visitors came from neighboring towns, including a Sunday School class from Hazleton, the girls all decked out in parasols and ribbons. The governor was represented, and the railroads, and the nation's leading newspapers. Over two thousand people gathered in Pottsville on this macabre holiday.

In West Patch, too, most of the homes were deserted. The miners and their families were drawn by a morbid compulsion to see the affair to its conclusion. The Flannerys, however, just completed a rosary in their rude dwelling and were kneeling in silence. Kitty began to sob.

"Now, now." Bridget slipped her plump arm around her daughter's shoulders. "Sure, it's in God's hands and the innocent one like Jimmy Boyle will go straight away to heaven."

"Oh, Mama. If I could have seen him only. If they would have given him my letters. Just to say how sorry I am."

"He knows that, surely. It's all we can do now to pray for his soul. And we done that."

Mike got up, walked to the window and looked out. "Awful quiet." He spoke almost to himself. Behind him, Kitty continued to cry softly.

Sean joined his father. "You goin' to the jailhouse, Pa?"

"I had a mind to."

"Can I come along?"

Captain Mike shook his head.

"But, Pa, I'm grown. I do a man's work in the mine. I want to go along now."

Bridget intervened. "No, Mike, no."

Mike looked down at his son thoughtfully. "All right. There'll be nothin' to see except a mob of people—some angry, some happy, some just curious. But it might be good you remember this day. Come on." He picked up his cap and the two men left by the front door, leaving Kitty and Bridget tearful behind them.

By ten o'clock, Sean and Mike were sifting through the mass of spectators standing outside the prison and glaring at the gray walls which hid the drama within. Brendan of Bally-cotton edged over to join the Flannerys.

Mike spoke to him.

"Any news?"

"There was talk of a pardon for Duffy, but nothin' come of it."

Mike nodded and then stood wordless and expectant. A policeman jostled him roughly as the hated "blacklegs" moved through the crowd to prevent trouble. On a nearby roof, several men squatted as lookouts and yelled down information to the mob.

Nothing stirred in the jail yard at the moment. Then soldiers filed out to form a hollow square around the newly constructed scaffold. Fresh timbers gleamed in the sun and the knotted hemp hung limp over the double trap. Below the structure, two soldiers jerked away two by fours to spring the doors. Satisfied that they would work, they replaced the sticks and stood at the ready. Nearby the reporters began to gather, accompanied by members of the trial juries, physicians, deputies, and other officials—perhaps two hundred in all.

Inside one of the prison's small cells, Father McDermott was concluding a private Mass. Following their confessions, the condemned men received Holy Communion for the last time. The priest covered his chalice and recited the final prayers. "Ite, Missa est." Go, you are dismissed. In a moment it was over and the prisoners were led away in pairs for the execution.

Roarity plucked Father McDermott's sleeve as he was being escorted out. "I've confessed my sins, Father, but I'd like to apologize to you for my conduct in church that time."

"I've forgotten it long ago, James."

"May God do the same." Roarity crossed himself.

The watchers on the rooftop shouted to those outside the walls. "Here they come! It's Roarity and Carroll!"

With no outward show of emotion, the two prisoners marched to the scaffold. Once there, they were granted a final statement.

Roarity was somewhat incoherent, trying to cram his denial into the few short minutes left to him. "Thomas Duffy has been convicted of giving me ten dollars for the shooting of a man I never saw—shooting him in Tamaqua—until I saw his name in the paper. I hope I am going to my Lord. And Thomas Duffy is a man that—I won't say for fear I might be lying—that I never seen him before I saw him in Pottsville jail and what I can say for him is this: I never heard him talking about Benjamin Yost, nor about the shooting affair, nor anything concerning the thing at all."

Carroll, alert and erect, his mustache carefully trimmed, was simple and direct. "I have nothing to say, gentlemen, only that I am innocent of the crime I am charged with."

Later, a written statement by Carroll was made public. It read:

Now, gentlemen, I do here confess to be innocent of the crime I am charged with. I never wished for the murder of Yost or any other person; or I never heard anyone say that they wanted murder committed, only Kerrigan, and I heard him often say that he would shoot Yost the first chance he got. I never knew Boyle or McGehan at the time, Now you can believe Kerrigan if you choose; but I hope if I have wronged any person they will forgive me as I forgive those who have so falsely belied me. I, as a dying man, have no animosity toward any person. I hope there will be no reflection thrown on my friends or family for this.

Father McDermott blessed both men and the white hoods were slipped over their heads. Handcuffed and with their arms strapped, they were guided to the trap doors. The ropes, which hung from the single crossbar, were snubbed about their necks. The throng outside heard the sharp slap as the boards were dropped. In the terrifying seconds that followed, there were only groans and curses and the distant words of the physician attesting the deaths.

"All over for Carroll and Roarity," the lookout shouted. "They're bringin' in McGehan and Boyle."

"May the Lord have mercy on all their souls," mumbled Brendan. Sean huddled close to his father, hoping for a miracle, and he could feel Captain Mike's trembling fingers biting into his arm.

At five minutes to eleven, a small procession moved along the brick wall, past the new wing of the prison. Behind the sheriff came Boyle and McGehan, each flanked by a deputy. Trailing them was a small detachment of Coal and Iron Police.

Jimmy Boyle carried a red rose in his left hand and he raised it to his nose as he walked. He seemed to be praying. McGehan paced beside him, carrying a brass crucifix in one hand and, in the other, a tiny porcelain statue of the Blessed Mother. In his lapel was a white rose.

They climbed unhesitatingly to the platform and then knelt as Father McDermott read the words of blessing from a book.

"Thank you, Father," said Jimmy. "Pray for us. And do give this rose to Kitty Flannery. Tell her my heart goes always with it."

"I'll do so, Jimmy. And you pray for me."

Burly Hugh McGehan stood up, looked down on the officials, and struggled with his final speech. "Gentlemen, I have nothing at all to say to you about my guilt or innocence, nor about them that left me in here, or them that done anything else to me. I done all that is in my power to save my soul." He stepped to the trapdoor and held his hands out for the cuffs.

Jimmy Boyle faced his audience and spoke deliberately and distinctly. "I have nothing to say, gentleman, only pretty much in the same way. Nothing as regards guilt or innocence. I forgive those that put me here and hope they will forgive me."

He took a step backward and felt the leather bands tighten around his arms, the bracelets click against the flesh of his wrists. As the hood was lowered, he turned toward McGehan and shouted, "Good-bye, old fellow. We'll die like men!" Hugh McGehan, already masked, nodded in agreement.

Then the priest and the sheriff moved back and the traps were sprung. The clatter was heard outside once again, followed by the frightened gasp of the crowd in unison and then the sobbing and the whispered litany.

Captain Mike held tightly to Sean and Brendan. His eyes misted over and he felt a new feeling creeping over him. Something spoke to him in his grief, awakened him. He realized for the first time that he was part of this tragedy—that these lives and deaths affected him. He sucked in his breath and tried to think.

But a hoarse cry broke his reverie. "Four down and two to go is the score. You, on the roof! Where's the rest?"

Mike recognized the voice before it was drowned in the laughter of the police and the mob's angry response. It was Taggart! Taggart, drunk and boastful, circled by police and gloating like a carrion bird.

Whatever force contained Captain Mike Flannery all these months and years now exploded. Rage dragged an unintelligible scream from his throat. As if in a dream, he was again at Cold Harbor and Vicksburg and careening through the Shenandoah Valley. Breaking from his companions, he plunged toward Taggart, split the police cordon, and spilled the mine boss with a diving tackle. The mob rolled forward, hampering the police and inscribing a circle around the two men. Helpless, the police drew back for reinforcements.

Taggart roared and thrust his knee up, catching Mike on the chin and rolling him backwards. As Mike tried to regain his feet, he was smashed with an elbow and felt Taggart's boot scrape his face. Scarcely noticing these blows, he bounced up, ducked a wild swing, and countered with a thumping punch to Taggart's stomach. He felt it thud home, heard the breath go out of his opponent. Like one possessed, he closed on Taggart's swaying figure. His mouth was bleeding and black dust caked his wild countenance. Leaping forward, he caught Taggart on the cheek with a right hand, stunning him. He buried his fist in the super's stomach again and crossed a left to his chin. Taggart wavered, like a barrel teetering. Mike swarmed over him, pommeling his body until he doubled over. Then he yelled again—madly, shrilly—and crumpled Taggart with a smash behind the ear. The mine boss crawled to one knee and held his hands in front of him, asking Mike to stop. His face was raw, bleeding; his clothes half torn from his body.

Captain Mike hovered over him, inhaling deeply, as the anger subsided. He shook his head to clear it, looked around, and saw the crowd for the first time. They cheered him lustily, slapped him on the back. There was a taste of blood in his mouth and, unconsciously, he wiped it away.

Taggart's voice was a broken sob. "I never meant to do it. God help me, Mike Flannery, I never meant to shoot your boy." He wept.

The outburst softened Mike. The thought of his son had not entered his mind and he now had a glimpse of his killer living with his guilt. Suddenly, he pitied him. Reaching down, he lifted him unsteadily to his feet. "I forgive you, Taggart. If I've any right to forgive, I forgive you. And may God forgive me for my own acts."

A path cleared swiftly and Mike walked through it. No police made a move to stop him, as he left the streets to the mad mourners. With Brendan and Sean he paced deliberately back to West Patch where Bridget met him and bathed his wounds.

"You're a bit old for these shenanigans, Mike Flannery," she scolded him. "But I'm proud of you all the same." And she kissed him on the forehead.

All day long, Mike sat by the window, watching the neighbors return and seeing the pain in their eyes. Father

McDermott delivered Jimmy Boyle's red rose and it lay on the table like a phantom relic. Mike's gaze wandered to it, thinking of the dead youth who would never return. The strange feeling came over him again. Reflecting on the recent fight, he realized that it was madness, that it solved nothing. Still, in those few savage movements, he was one with the miners. He shared something with them, if only a rash hatred. Before he had always struggled alone, suffered alone. What did it all mean?

The day wore on and darkness descended upon the valley, bringing no peace, but only sorrow and despair. Mike watched the sun disappear, saw the lamps leap to life in dozens of curtained windows. He turned to see his family regarding him with apprehension.

"Mike," said Bridget, "it's not like you to cut us out. What is it?"

"I don't know. If I tried to tell you, it would come out a jumble of words like 'justice,' and 'duty' and 'unity' and things that have no definitions." He jerked his hat from the hook and started out.

Bridget's eyes never left him as she quietly ordered Sean, "Go along with your pa, son."

Hearing no disagreement, Sean obeyed, striding mutely beside his father. In silence they walked through the patch which was as quiet as the new graves. On either side loomed the dark hills spiked with trees. The road twisted beneath their feet. From Pottsville they heard the wheeze of the mine machinery and the familiar rolling din of exploding powder. Work as usual. The earth couldn't grieve, nor the pit remember.

At random they followed the course of the Schuylkill for a while and then took a footpath into the woods. An owl hooted in the void. Twigs snapped beneath their feet and weird shapes emerged in the darkness. On they walked in silence.

All at once they noticed a weak flicker of light and they heard voices in whispered conversation. Moving forward, Mike saw that a small group of miners—two dozen, perhaps— were gathered around a dying fire. Brendan was there, and Danny Kelley, and some others he recognized. They jumped at the sound of his footsteps.

Brendan stepped forward. "Mike! What brings you out here?"

"A walk. Then curiosity. But what about yourselves?"

Brendan smiled. It was strange to see that someone could still smile. "We are honest men, Mike, as you can see, but since we can't meet in the town hall, this place is as good as any."

"You're organizing the miners?"

"Reorganizing them."

"But," Mike shook his head in disbelief, "but the papers say the Mollies are crushed, gone."

"And so they are. But we aren't ground under yet. You remember your Gospels, Mike? When the Apostles were threatened, didn't they hide in the room so, and the Christians went to the catacombs."

Mike recalled the passage from his seminary days, saw it swimming before him. "Now when it was late the same day, the first of the week, and the doors were shut, where the disciples were gathered together for fear of the Jews, Jesus came and stood in their midst and said: Peace be to you." He could almost feel this presence now and suddenly he realized his vocation. After all these years, perhaps this was his calling. Numbly, he sat down.

"This is my boy, Sean. You know him, I think?"

There were nods and handshakes, then a long silence.

Brendan broke it. "We've no plans, Mike, no leaders. All we have is a great wrong upon us and a great fear for our lives and our families and our future."

"The Mollies were a mistake, Brendan. First, it was wrong. Then it was alone. We've been isolated. The others didn't come in and didn't support them. The press was against them, and the Church."

The circle of men listened attentively to Mike, not interrupting.

"We don't have to go it alone. There are thousands of us—here and elsewhere. And the mineowners are not all Gowens to spit on us. Some are decent men, men who will listen."

"You talkin' union, Captain Mike?"

He nodded. "No bloodshed and no violence. A peaceful union like before."

Brendan shook his head. "It failed before. Bates tried it. And Siney. You haven't forgotten the Workingmen's Benevolent Association or the Miners and Laborers?"

"Every cause fails many times and this is no different. Before anything succeeds, it has to suffer. We've suffered and we're still brothers. This time we'll succeed—together. But patience. And peaceful means. These will be our arms."

The men looked around the circle, then slowly and confidently, they reached forth and clasped hands. Sean felt his father's huge fist clamped around his own. It was trembling, but the grip was firm.

Epilogue

In the years that followed, the mine unions were born, but not without further struggles and further sacrifice. In the twentieth century, responsible union leadership and intelligent management response have compromised on better working conditions.

Since the Flannerys have merely a fictional existence, we can only speculate on their futures. Most of the other characters, however, outlived these few chapters.

James McParlan (sometimes written McParlin or McParland) rose to prominence as chief of the Pinkerton's Denver bureau and later tangled with the famous Clarence Darrow in a celebrated Colorado mining case. Franklin B. Gowen ended his life alone—a suicide. In the Mammoth Vein country, the miners attributed his death to a haunting sense of guilt.

With the passing of Jimmy Boyle and the nineteen others who marched to the gallows, the Molly Maguires were said to be finished. Their reputation, however, survived. One of the victims—Alexander Campbell of Summit Hill, who was executed for the murder of John P. Jones—protested the verdict and, placing his hand on the wall of his cell, promised his jailers that the imprint would always remain there as proof of his innocence. Despite washing and repainting, the impression of that hand remained until 1931 when the cell was replastered.

From such deeds, legends are born.

❧

The principal events of this novel are true and happened very much as herein related. The courtroom dialogue is accurately reproduced from court records and newspaper accounts. Some incidents and some personalities have been telescoped for the sake of brevity.

Afterword

The story of the Flannery family is shared by many immigrant groups who came to the United States looking for a better life. The Irish, fleeing from oppression and famine in Ireland, found similar conditions in many of the places they settled. Signs in Boston establishments in the late eighteenth and early nineteenth centuries spoke eloquently: "Irish need not apply." In the coal mines as in other heavy industry, owners sought to retain control not only of the workplace but of all aspects of the workers' lives, and the Irish were only one of the groups to suffer from this control.

The Molly Maguires were a desperate answer to desperate times, and blood was shed, crimes committed on both sides of the question. As the reader becomes involved in the lives of the Flannerys and their neighbors, in the secret codes and violence of the Maguires on one side and the owners on the other, many questions arise that can provoke thoughtful discussion. For those who might like to explore these and other questions, look at the web page for *Rebels in the Shadows* at http://www.pitt.edu/~press/goldentrianglebooks.